Praise For *Sir*

*S*ing Me Your *Scar.*   ⌐ in the mind's
eye in a kaleidosc ⸍e of darkness and
wonder. Walters is impressive.

—Laird Barron, author of *The Croning* and *The Beautiful Thing That Awaits Us All*

Damien Angelica Walters writes prose as
sharp as a scalpel. With surgical precision, she slices through her characters' veneers to lay bare the secret scars underneath, the knots of fear and desire twisting them. The women and men in these stories struggle against their own, oddly-beautiful damage, and even when they succumb to it, the narrative is never less than compelling. Anatomist of dreams and nightmares, Walters is a writer to watch.

—John Langan, author of *The Wide, Carnivorous Sky and Other Monstrous Geographies*

Sing Me Your Scars

www.apexbookcompany.com

Sing Me Your Scars

stories by

Damien Angelica Walters

An Apex Publications Book
Lexington, Kentucky

This anthology is a work of fiction. All the characters and events portrayed in these stories are either fictitious or are used fictitiously.

Sing Me Your Scars
ISBN: 978-1-937009-28-1
Copyright © 2015 by Damien Angelica Walters
Cover Sketch © 2015 by Angela McDermott
Cover Design and Layout © 2015 Juliana M. Hernandez
Typography © 2015 by Maggie Slater

Published by Apex Publications, LLC
PO Box 24323
Lexington, K.Y. 40524
www.apexbookcompany.com

For Jeremiah and Chloe

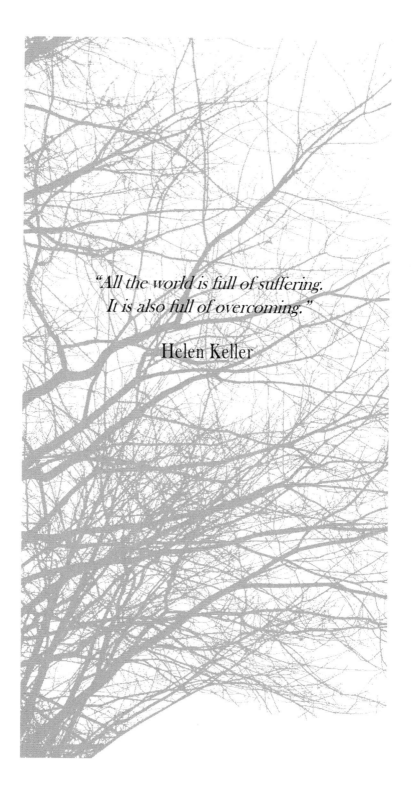

"*All the world is full of suffering.*
It is also full of overcoming."

Helen Keller

Table of Contents

☙ ❧

PART I: HERE

Sing Me Your Scars   3
All the Pieces We Leave Behind   17
Girl, With Coin   29
Paskutinis Iliuzija (The Last Illusion)   39
Glass Boxes and Clockwork Gods   51
Sugar, Sin, and Nonsuch Henry   59

PART II: AND THE NOW

Running Empty in a Land of Decay   75
Scarred   78
The Taste of Tears in a Raindrop   87
Always, They Whisper   99
Dysphonia in D Minor   110
Shall I Whisper to You of Moonlight,
    of Sorrow, of Pieces of Us?   121
Immolation: A Love Story   128

PART III: AND AWAY

Melancholia in Bloom   135
Iron and Wood, Nail and Bone   143
And All the World Says Hush   148
They Make of You a Monster   150
Paper Thin Roses of Maybe   159
Grey in the Gauge of His Storm   167
Like Origami in Water   176

Acknowledgements

When Maurice Broaddus approached me at Killercon to talk about a possible collection, I confess I didn't believe him at first. Oh I believed his intent, but my dark little pessimistic heart said really, do you think anyone would want a collection from *you*? Sorry, Maurice.

I believed him when he emailed me after the convention. Mostly.

So, Maurice, I owe you a huge thank you for setting the ball in motion. And to Jason Sizemore and Linda Epstein, thank you for making this a reality.

I love short fiction. I love reading it and writing it. It's a playground of possibility that gives me the freedom to write in any genre, style, tense, or voice. Over the past few years, I've had the opportunity to work with some fantastic editors, and I'd like to thank those who originally published the reprints in this collection: John Joseph Adams, Scott Andrews, Andy Cox, John Klima, Jonathan and Michele Laden, Brit Mandelo, An Owomoyela, Rhonda Parrish, Julia Rios, Lynne Thomas, Elise Tobler, Brian White, and Ken Wood.

To my beta readers: Elise, Jake, Ken, Brenda, Rhonda, and Peter. Thank you a gazillion times over. My stories wouldn't be the same without your input. If I've left anyone out, the mistake is mine, not yours.

Thank you to Laird Barron and John Langan for reading the collection in its early stages and for offering your words of support. Beyond measure, you have my gratitude.

And to Al, thank you for your love and support. It means the world to me.

So, the stories… Are they any good? That's not for me to decide. My ownership of these tales is done. They belong to you, the reader, now. Thank you for walking through the playground with me. Good or bad, these were the stories I had inside me at the time of the telling.

Damien Angelica Walters
2014

Part I

Here

Sing Me
Your Scars

ᚼ ᚼ

This is not my body.
   Yes, there are the expected parts—arms, legs, hips, breasts—each in its proper place and of the proper shape. Is he a monster, a madman, a misguided fool? I don't know. I don't want to know. But this is not my body.

The rot begins, as always, around the stitches. This time, the spots of greyish-green appear on the left wrist, and there is an accompanying ache, but not in the expected way. It feels as though there is a great disconnect between mind and flesh, a gap that yearns to close but cannot. I say nothing, but there is no need; Lillian's weeping says it with more truth than words.
   The hands are hers.
   "Please don't show him yet. Please," she whispers. "I'm not ready."
   "I must," I say. "You will be fine."
   "Please, please, wait until after the party."
   I ignore her. I have learned the hard way that hiding the rot is not acceptable, and while the flesh may be hers, the pain is mine and mine alone. I remember hearing him offer an explanation, but the words, the theories, were too complex for me to understand. I suspect that was his intention.
   Lillian will still be with us; she is simply grasping for an excuse, any excuse at all. I understand her fear, but the rot could destroy us all.
   My stride is long. Graceful. Therese was a dancer, and she taught me the carriage of a lady. I pass old Ilsa in the hallway, and

she offers a distracted nod over the mound of bed linens she carries. All the servants are busy with preparations for the upcoming annual party, which I'm not allowed to attend, of course.

I wonder what sort of fiction he has spun to the servants. Am I an ill cousin, perhaps, or someone's cast-off bastard that he has taken in? Either way, I'm certain they call him the good doctor, but they're not here at night. They don't know everything.

They never speak to me, nor do they offer anything more than nods or waves of the hand, and none of them can see my face through the veil I must wear when I venture beyond my rooms. All my gowns have high necklines and long, flowing sleeves; not a trace of flesh is exposed.

For my safety, he says. They will not understand. They will be afraid and people in fear often act in a violent manner. His mouth never says what sort of violence he expects, but his eyes do.

When I knock on the half-open door to his study, he glances up from his notebooks. I shut the door behind me, approach his desk slowly, and hold out Lillian's hand.

"Oh, Victoria," he says, shaking his head. "I had hoped we were past this. This configuration is as close to perfect as I could hope."

I bite my tongue. Victoria is not my name, simply a construct.

I asked him once why he had done such a thing; he called me an ungrateful wretch and left his handprint on my cheek. I wonder if he even knows why. Perhaps the answer is so ugly he has buried it deep inside.

Without another word, he leads me to the small operating theater, unlocks the door, and steps aside to let me enter first. The room smells of antiseptic and gauze, but it's far better than the wet flesh reek of the large theater. My visual memories are vague, but the smell will not leave, no matter how hard I try to forget.

I sit on the edge of the examination table without prompting. His face is grim, studied, as he inspects the wrist, and even though his touch is gentle, I watch his eyes for signs of anger. I know the rot is not my fault, but innocence is no guard against rage.

He makes a sound deep in his throat. Of sorrow? Condemnation?

Lillian weeps, then begs, then prays. None of which will make any difference.

The rot binds us to him as the stitches bind them to me. A prison, not of bars, but circumstance. I have entertained thoughts of the scissors and the thread, the undoing to set us free, but I have no wish to die again, and neither do the others. While not perfect, this existence is preferable. And what if we did not die? What if our pieces remained alive and sentient? A crueler fate I cannot imagine.

He scrapes a bit of the rot away, revealing a darker patch beneath. When he lets out a heavy sigh, I note the absence of liquor on his breath.

He busies himself with the necessary preparations, and Lillian begins to cry again. The others remain silent. He paints the wrist with an anesthetic, which surprises me. My tears have never stopped him from his work. I close my eyes and feel pressure. Hear the blades snipping through the stitches. Smell the foul scent of decay as it reaches out from beneath.

He places the hand in a small metal tray, then coats the remaining flesh in an ointment that smells strongly of pine and wraps it in gauze.

"We shall know in a few days."

Diana's worry is as strong as mine. Lillian tries to speak but cannot force the words through her sorrow and fear.

When the anesthetic wears off, the skin gives a steady thump of pain from beneath the gauze and I do my best to ignore it.

"At least it was only the one," Grace says.

"You wouldn't understand," Lillian snaps.

"What if it spreads?" Diana asks.

Molly mutters something I cannot decipher, but it makes Lillian weep again.

"Hush," says Therese. "Remember Emily? She had reason to weep. You do not."

Sophie laughs. The sound is cruel. Hard.

"Stop, please, all of you," I finally say. "I need to sleep. To heal."

Heal is not the right term, perhaps *remain* would be better.

"I'm sorry, Kimberly," Lillian says softly.

The sound of my real name hurts, but not as much as the false one. At least Kimberly is, was, real.

The rest apologize as well, even Sophie, and fall silent. I toss and turn beneath the blankets and eventually slip from my bed. The others say nothing when I open the small door hidden behind a tapestry on the wall. The passageway is narrow and dusty, and spiders scurry out of my way; it travels around the east wing of the house—the only part of the house where I'm allowed—then leads to the central part, the main house. There are small covered holes here and there that open to various rooms, to carpets my feet will never touch and sofas I will never recline upon. The passageway also goes to the west wing of the house, but the rooms are unused and the furniture nothing more than cloth covered shapes in the darkness. The only doors I have found lead to bedrooms—mine, his, and one other designed for guests, although we never have guests stay—and one near the music room.

There is, as always, a race in the heartbeat, a dryness to the mouth, when I creep from the passage and make my way to the servants' entrance. The air outside is cold enough to take my breath away as I follow the narrow path that leads to the gate in the outer wall. There is another path that leads down the hill and into the town, but the gate is locked.

I pretend that one day I will walk through the gate and down that path. Leave this house behind; leave him behind for good. But if I ran away and the rot returned, who would fix me? The rot would not stop until it consumed me whole.

I know this for truth because he left it alone the first time to see what would happen, and the rot crept its way up until he had no choice but to remove the entire arm. Her name was Rachael, and he removed both arms so he could then attach a matching set.

Most of the windows in the town are dark. The church's steeple rises high, a glint of moonlight on the spire. I have heard the servants talk about the market, the church. Beyond the town, a road winds around a bend and disappears from sight.

My parents' farm is half a day's travel from the town by horse and carriage. It would be a long, difficult walk but not impossible.

I wonder if Peter, my eldest brother, has asked for Ginny's hand in marriage yet. I wonder if Tom, younger than I by ten months, has stopped growing (when I fell ill, he already towered over all of us). I wonder if my mother still sings as she churns butter. And my father...the last thing I remember are the tears in his eyes. I hope he has found a way to smile again; I wish I could see them all once more, even if only from a distance.

I wait for someone to speak, to mention escape and freedom, but they remain silent. After a time, I return to my bed and press my hand to Molly's chest. The heart belongs to someone else, someone not us. Sometimes I think I feel her presence, like a ghostly spirit in an old house, but she never speaks. Perhaps there is not enough of her here to have a voice. Perhaps she simply refuses to speak.

I wish I knew her name.

Although the stump shows no more signs of rot, he doesn't replace Lillian's hand. It makes dressing difficult at best, but I manage.

After supper, when all the servants have gone, I join him in the music room. I sing the songs he has taught me. Melodies which were strange and awkward at first now flow with ease; foreign words that fumbled on my tongue now taste of familiarity.

He accompanies me on the piano he says belonged to his mother. Only two songs tonight, and after the second, he waves his hand in dismissal, and I notice the red in his eyes and the tremble in his fingers. Perhaps he is worried about the party.

When he comes to my room in the middle of the night, I hide my surprise. He usually doesn't touch me unless I'm whole, but by now I know what is expected, so I raise my chemise and part Therese's legs. When he kisses my neck, I pretend it belongs to someone else. Anyone else. The others whisper to me of nonsense as a distraction. Thankfully, he doesn't take long.

After he leaves, I use Lillian's finger to trace the stitches. They divide us into sections like countries on a map. The head, neck, and shoulders are mine; the upper torso, Molly's; the lower torso, Grace's; Diana, the arms; Lillian, the hand; Therese, the legs and feet; Sophie, the scalp and hair.

I make all the pieces of this puzzle move, I feel touches or insult upon them, but they never feel as if they belong completely to me. He may know how everything works on the outside, but he doesn't know that they are here with me on the inside, too. We plan to keep it this way.

Once a week, in the small operating theater, he has me strip and he inspects all the stitches, all the parts. He checks my heart and listens to me breathe. I hate the feel of his eyes upon me; it's far worse than enduring his weight in my bed.

Not long after he brought me back, I tried to stab myself with a knife. At the last moment, I held back and only opened a small wound above the left breast. Stitches hold it closed now.

He says the mind of all things, from the smallest insect to the largest animal, desires life, no matter the flesh. He says I am proof of this.

But it was Emily's doing. She was with me from the beginning, and she was always kind, always patient. She helped me stay sane. Like a mother, she whispered soft reassurances to me when I cried; told me I was not a monster when I insisted otherwise; promised me everything would be all right. She taught me how to strip the farm from my speech.

He tried hard to save her, carving away at the rot a bit at a time, but in the end he could not halt its progress. She screamed when he split apart the stitches. I did, too. Sometimes I feel as if her echo is still inside me and it offers a small comfort. Therese is kind, but I preferred my walk when it carried Emily's strength.

"I will unlock your door when the party is over," he says.

I nod.

"You will stay silent?"

"Yes."

"I would not even hold this party if not for my father's insufferable tradition. I curse him for beginning it in the first place, and I should have ended it when he died."

I know nothing of his father other than a portrait in the music room. He, too, was a doctor. I wonder if he taught his son how to make me.

The key turns in the door. I sit, a secret locked in with the shadows.

Even from my room, I can hear the music. The laughter. I creep in the passageway with small, quiet steps, extinguish my lamp, and swing open the spyhole. The year before, I was recovering and did not know about the passageway; the year before that, I was not here.

I twine a lock of Sophie's hair around my finger and watch the men and women spinning around on the dance floor, laughing with goblets of wine in hand, talking in animated voices. He is there, resplendent in a dark suit, but I don't allow my eyes to linger on him for too long. This smiling man is as much a construct as I am.

"I had a gown like that blue one," Grace says. "Oh, how I miss satin and lace."

"Please," Lillian says. "Let us go back. I can't bear to see this. The reminder hurts too much."

"Hush," Molly says.

"I wish we could join them," Diana says.

Sophie says, "Perhaps he will bring us some wine later. And look, look at the food."

Therese makes a small sound. "Look at the way they dance. Clumsy, so clumsy."

I sway back and forth, my feet tracing a pattern not from Therese, but a dance from my childhood. I remember the harvest festival, the bonfire, the musicians. My father placed my feet atop his to teach me the steps, and then he spun me around and around until we were both too dizzy to stand.

Therese laughs, but there is no mockery in the sound. I close my eyes, lost in the memory of my father's arms around me, how safe and secure I always felt. I would give anything to feel that way again.

The music stops, and my eyes snap open. A young woman in a dark blue gown approaches the piano, sits, and begins to play. The music is filled with tiny notes that reach high in the air then swoop back down, touching on melancholia. It's the most beautiful thing I have ever heard. Everyone falls silent, even Lillian.

Then I see him watching the girl at the piano. His brow is creased; his mouth soft. I hear a strange sound from Sophie. She recognizes the intensity of his gaze. As a kindness, I let go of her hair. Does he covet this girl's arms? Her hair? Her face?

Lillian begins to weep again, and it doesn't take long for the rest to join her. All except Sophie. She never cries.

"He will not," I say.

"He will do whatever he wants. You know that," Sophie says.

"She is not sick," Grace says.

"Neither was I," Sophie hisses. "He saw me in the Hargrove market. He gave me *that* look, then I woke up here."

"But you do not know for certain," Therese says. "The influenza took so many."

"I was not sick." Sophie's voice is flat. Then, she says nothing more.

Hargrove is even further away than my parents' farm. I bend my head forward, and Sophie's hair spills down, all chestnut brown and thick curls. My hair was straight and thin, best suited for tucking beneath roughspun scarves, not hanging free, but still I cried when he replaced it.

He is drunk again. His voice is loud. Angry. I pull the sheets up to my shoulders and hope he doesn't come to visit. When he is drunk, it takes longer.

Sometimes I want to sneak into his study and take one of the bottles and hide it in my room. On nights when I can still hear my mother saying my name; when I can remember the illness that confined me to my bed and eventually took my life; when I recall the confusion when I woke here and knew something was wrong.

But those nights happen less and less, and I'm afraid I will forget my mother's voice completely. Would she even recognize me with Sophie's hair in place of my own? Would she run screaming?

On Sunday morning, I creep through the passageway. Step outside. The servants have the day off, and he has gone to mass. Even here, I can hear voices in song. I remember these songs from my own church where I sang with the choir. I have never known if he heard me somehow and chose me because of my voice, but I remember seeing him on the farm in my fifteenth year when Peter broke his arm, two years before the influenza epidemic.

"We should leave," Sophie says.

"Yes, we should run far away," Lillian says.

"And where would we go?" Molly asks.

"Anywhere."

Therese laughs. "And who will fix us if we rot?"

"Better that we rot away to nothing than remain here," Sophie says.

The others start speaking over each other, denying her words. In truth, I do not know what I want. When I head back inside, the voices outside are still singing and those inside still arguing.

Days pass, then weeks. The stump remains rot free, but he says nothing of it, only nods when he does his inspection. He spends his days in the town, ministering to the sick. I spend mine in the library, reading of wars and dead men and politics. Rachael taught me how to read; now Sophie helps when I find myself stuck on a word.

"Wake up."

His voice is rough, scented with whiskey.

"Now?"

"Yes, hurry."

"No, oh, no," someone says as we approach the small operating theater, but I cannot tell who it is.

He tears away my chemise. Pushes me down on the table.

"But there is nothing wrong," I say.

"Don't let him do this," Lillian screams. "Please, don't let him do this to me."

He lifts a blade. I grab his forearm, dig Lillian's nails in hard enough to make him wince.

"Please, no."

He slaps me across the face with his free hand. The others are shrieking, shouting. Lillian is begging, pleading, screaming for me to make him stop. I grab his arm again and try to swing Therese's legs off the table. He slaps me twice more and presses a sharp-smelling cloth over my mouth and nose. I hold my breath until my chest tightens; he pushes the cloth harder.

I breathe in, and everything goes grey—*I'm sorry, Lillian. So sorry.*—then black.

I wake in my bed, the sheets tucked neatly around me. The others are weeping, and Lillian is gone. I choke back my tears because I don't wish to frighten the newcomer.

"What has happened to me?" she asks. Her voice is small and trembling.

"What is your name?" I ask.

"Anna," she says.

"Welcome to madness," Sophie says, her voice strangely flat.

"Hush," Molly says.

"Who is that? What is this? Please, I want to go home."

"I told you," Sophie says, still in that strange, lifeless tone. "We should have run away."

"Where am I?" Anna says. "How did I get here?"

I try to explain, but nothing I say helps. Nothing can make it right, and in the end, we are all weeping, even Sophie, and that frightens me more than I could have imagined.

I don't see him for several days. The music room remains dark, the door to the operating theater locked. I retreat to the library, lose myself in books, and pretend not to hear Anna cry. We have all tried to offer support, but she rebuffs every attempt so there is nothing to do but wait. Eventually, she will accept the way things are now, the way we've all been forced into acceptance.

There are no signs of rot along the new stitches. They're uneven both in length and spacing—not nearly as neat as the others—but they hold firm. Anna's hands are delicate with long slender fingers, the skin far paler than Diana's. The weight is wrong; they're far too light, as if I'm wearing gloves instead of hands.

I miss Lillian so very much. I didn't even have a chance to say goodbye.

When he enters the library, I notice first his disheveled clothes, then the red of his eyes. He tosses my book aside, drags me to the music room, and shoves me toward the piano.

"Tell her to play."

Everyone falls silent. Surely we have heard him wrong.

"I don't understand."

He steps close enough for me to smell the liquor. "Tell Anna to play," he says, squeezing each word out between clenched teeth.

I sit down and thump on the keys, the notes painful enough to make me grit my teeth. I poke and prod, but Anna is hiding the knowledge deep inside, and I cannot pull it free. I offer a tentative smile even though I want to scream.

"Shall I sing instead?"

He groans and pulls me from the bench. The skirts tangle and twist, and I stumble. He digs his fingers into my shoulders, brings my face close to his. "Did you truly believe I didn't know? I have heard you speak to them. I know they are in there with you. You tell her to play. Or else."

"Never," Anna says.

Therese's legs are no longer strong enough to hold us up, and I sink to the floor. He smiles, the gesture like a whip. Eventually, he stalks from the room, and I sit with Diana's arms around me.

Sophie hisses, "Bastard."

"You must teach me how to play," I tell Anna.

"I will not."

"Please, you must. If you don't, he will kill you."

"It doesn't matter. I am already dead."

"But he may kill us all, and we don't want to die."

The others chime in in agreement.

"I do not care," Anna says. "I will give him nothing. He killed me. Don't you understand? He killed me!"

"Yes, I do," says Sophie. "We do. But this is what we have now."

"I do not want this. It is monstrous, and you, all of you, you're as dead as I am."

"Please," I say. "Teach me something, anything that will make him happy. I'm begging you, please."

She doesn't respond.

Three more trips to the music room. Three more refusals that leave me with a circlet of bruises around the arms; red marks on my cheeks in the shape of his hand; more bruises on the soft skin between breasts and belly. The others scream at Anna when he strikes me, but she doesn't give in.

She is strong. Stronger than any of us.

The fourth trip. The fourth refusal. He pulls me from the bench with his hands around my neck. His fingers squeeze tighter and tighter until spots dance in my eyes and when he lets go, I fall to the floor gasping for air as he walks away without even a backward glance.

I wake to find his face leering over mine. I bite back the tears, begin to lift my chemise, and he slaps my hand.

"If you cannot make her play, I will find someone else who will." He traces the stitches just above the collarbone, spins on his heel, and lurches from the room.

I sit in the darkness and let the tears flow. I don't want to die again. I will not.

I creep into the passageway and make my way into the kitchen. Cheese, bread, a few apples. An old cloak hangs from a hook near the servants' entrance. I slip it on and pull up the hood before I step outside. The air is cold enough to sting my cheeks, too cold for the thin cloak, but I head toward the gate, searching the ground for a rock large enough to break the lock.

Perhaps my mother will scream, perhaps my father and brothers will threaten me with violence, but they cannot hurt me more than he has.

I'm five steps away from the gate when he grabs me from behind. All the air rushes from my lungs. I draw another breath to scream, and his hand covers my mouth. He leans close to my ear.

"I had such high hopes for you. Perhaps I will have better luck with the next one."

I fight to break free. The gate is so close. So close.

He laughs. "Do you have any idea what they would do to you? Even your own parents would tear you limb from limb and toss you into the fire. If I didn't need the rest of them, I'd let you go so you could find out."

He presses a cloth to my mouth, and I try not to breathe in.

I fail.

I wake in the large operating theater. The smell is blood and decay, pain and suffering. I scream and pound on the door, but it's barred from the outside. I sink down and cover my eyes; I don't want to see the equipment, the tools, the knives, and the reddish-brown stains. There are no windows, no hidden doors, no secret passageways. There is no hope.

I have no idea how much time passes before he comes. "This is your last chance," he says. "Will you play?"

"No," Anna says.

"Please, please," the others beg.

"I will not."

"She will not play," I say, my voice little more than a whisper. He smiles. "I thought not." He closes the door again.

Does he mean to leave us locked here until we die? I bang on the door until tiny smears of blood mark the wood, then I curl up into a small ball in the corner.

I wake when he opens the door again and drags something in wrapped in a sheet. No, not a something. A body. I lurch to my feet.

"No, no, you cannot do this. Please."

"I can do whatever I want. I made you, and I can unmake you."

He approaches me with another cloth in his hand. I know if I breathe this time, I will never wake again. Sophie is shrieking. They all are.

I stumble against a table and instruments clatter to the floor with a metallic tangle. I reach blindly with Anna's hand, find a handle, and swing. He steps into the blade's path, and it sinks deep into his chest. He drops the cloth; his mouth opens and closes, opens and closes again, then he collapses to the floor as if boneless. Anna lets out a sound of triumph, but I cannot speak, cannot breathe, cannot move.

"No, no," Sophie shouts. "What have you done?"

Therese and Grace scream, Diana lets out a keening wail, Molly babbles incoherencies that sound of madness, and all the while, Anna laughs.

His eyes flutter shut, and his chest rises, falls, rises. I drop to his side and pull the blade free, grimacing at the blood that fountains forth. His eyes seek mine. His mouth moves, and it sounds as if he is trying to say, "I'm sorry," but perhaps that is only what I wish he would say.

Nonetheless, I say, "I'm sorry, too."

Then, I begin to cut.

"Thank you," Anna whispers, right before the blade touches the last stitch and she is set free. I close my eyes for a brief moment to wish her well on her journey, but there is not enough time to mourn her properly.

My stitches are clumsy, ugly, but they seem sturdy enough for now. His hands are too large, the movements awkward, but gloves will hide them, and soon I will know how to make everything work the way it's supposed to.

He whispers he will never tell us how. We laugh because we know he will eventually; he will not want his creation, his knowledge, to fall apart or to rot away and die. He mutters obscenities, names, and threats, but we ignore him.

We are not afraid of him anymore.

In the ballroom, I set fire to the drapes and wait long enough to see the flames spread to the ceiling and across the floor in a roiling carpet of destruction.

"Where shall we go?" Therese asks.

"I don't know," I say.

Sophie gives a small laugh. "We can go anywhere we wish."

The heat of the blaze follows us out. The air is thick with the stench of burning wood and the death of secrets. The promise of freedom. We pause at the gate and glance back. A section of the roof caves in with a rush of orange sparks, flames curl from the windows, and the fire's rage growls and shrieks.

When we hear shouts emerge from the town below, we slip into the shadows. This is our, *my*, body, and I will be careful. I will keep us safe.

All the Pieces
We Leave Behind

❧ ❧

Meg locked the door behind the last customer and flipped the hanging sign to *Closed*. Despite her aching feet and stiff lower back, this was her favorite time of the night. The shelves of the bookstore shimmered with what the customers had left behind, a mix of excitement and happiness. The rug in the children's section gave off a soft glow, and the air was redolent with the scent of sunshine after a long rain.

On her way out, she trailed her fingers across a shelf and smiled. She wondered, not for the first time, how people could bear to work in offices where the internal politics turned everything sticky and grasping. Then again, most people weren't even aware of what lingered around them.

The early autumn air held a slight chill, a promise of the colder nights to come. A homeless man sleeping in a puddle of shadow next to the steps of a building didn't stir as Meg tucked a few dollar bills into the cup at his side, avoiding the strands of dejection that smelled of sour milk and dangled from his clothing like lifeless tentacles.

Halfway to her apartment, she turned a corner and walked into a red and blue whirl of police lights cordoning off the entire street. Behind the blockade, she saw an ambulance, several uniformed officers, and a young man sitting on the curb with his wrists cuffed. Regret pooled around his feet; his features were obscured behind a veil of sorrow the color of brackish water.

"You'll have to go around another way, ma'am," an officer said.

"Thank you. Please be safe," she said as she turned around.

If she went around the block, she'd have to walk past the bars on Linwood Street and the want, the need, and the sad desperation made the sidewalk a dangerous place. She did her best to avoid places awash in negativity, like a coffee shop first thing in the morning with too many people rushing, glancing at their watches, and grumbling at the lines. All of it made for a storm of chaos that spiraled in the air, dropping tiny bits like confetti. The last time she'd dared, she'd left with a migraine.

But to avoid the bars, she'd have to go another block out of her way. A tiny twinge in her back made the decision for her. Just this once, she'd take the risk; if she walked fast, maybe it wouldn't be so bad.

Even through the closed doors, the music from the bars pushed out into the street, a steady thump of drums and a whine of guitar. A handful of people congregated on the sidewalk, smoking and speaking in hushed tones. A neon glow danced on the pavement, but the light held no cheer. The very walls pushed out a strange sort of sadness, sticky with lies and sharp with need. The air was heavy with the smell of beer and a hint of stale vomit, and beneath, a smell like citrus left too long on the vine.

She kept as close to the curb as possible, but the concrete tugged at her feet, trying to lure her in with false promises of happiness in martini glasses, of conversation in slurred words, of love in a stranger's tangled sheets.

She sidestepped a broken patch of pavement, and someone shoved into her from behind, propelling her forward. She stumbled, arms flailing. Her palms met a hard, muscled chest, and hands grabbed her upper arms.

She glanced up into striking blue eyes. Strong cheekbones. A cleft chin. A handsome face, but beyond the blue of his eyes, there was nothing. No compassion, no anger, only a vast emptiness. He offered a smile that held as little emotion as his gaze.

Dark grey swirled around him as if he were wrapped in a shroud. Her hands, still resting on his chest, were barely visible. Her palms tingled. A thick smell, like char mixed with petroleum, filled her nose, and she felt something she'd never felt before, something dark and oily that spoke in a language she didn't understand, was never meant to understand. Her breath caught in her throat. His grip tightened.

She wrenched away from his touch, and threads of grey pulled free from the shroud with a wet tear. Mocking laughter carried in the air as she staggered away, brushing her hands together. Tiny bits of grey dislodged and dropped to the pavement, yet more clung to her skin, creeping across like a legion of insects; her flesh, their battlefield.

She half-ran, half-walked the rest of the way home. Once inside her apartment, she slammed the dead bolt shut and stripped on her way to the bathroom. She turned the water as hot as she could stand it and stood under the spray, her hands shaking, for a long time. She soaped up again and again but could still feel it on her skin, a vile coating like a sheath of sorrow. With a soft sob, she grabbed a washcloth and started scrubbing her arms.

When she finally emerged, her skin was pink and throbbing. No traces of grey remained that she could find, yet the strange sensation lingered, and every time she closed her eyes, she saw the man's empty gaze.

Listen to me…

Meg sat up straight in bed and fumbled for the light. She'd heard something. A voice, a whisper. She walked through her apartment, checking the locks on the windows and the door. When finished, she crept back into bed, but gave up trying to fall asleep when the edges of the sky began to lighten.

In the morning, one of her frequent customers came into the bookstore with her three children. The little ones headed straight for the toy box while their mother browsed the romance section. The youngest child pulled several books from the shelf and more tumbled to the floor in a flurry of paper. Irritation bloomed inside Meg like a dark rose, and her skin prickled.

The stupid little fool. And will his mother pay for the books if he tears them? No, she'll probably slide it back on the shelf when she thinks I'm not looking.

Meg clamped one hand over her mouth. Shame bloomed in her cheeks. Where had that come from? The prickling faded away.

She stuck out her hands and flipped them over. No grey. She bent down, lifted her skirt to her thighs, and inspected her legs. No grey there, either.

She shook her head. She was imagining things; that was all. She just needed a good night's sleep.

On her way home, Meg turned down Linwood Street. The Friday night crowd was a far cry from the previous night. The sidewalks were filled with people standing and shouting loudly over the music bleeding out into the night from the open doors, and a heavy cloud of cigarette smoke hung in the air. Lust dripped in silvery streaks from hips and thighs like mercury from a broken thermometer. Of the man in the shroud, there was no sign.

She stepped closer, and a man stepped in front of her, blocking her path. "Hey, lady, you look lonely. How about a drink?"

"No, thank you," she said.

"Just one?" He smiled, moving close enough that she could smell the beer on his breath.

Disgusting.

Her skin started to tingle. Her hands curled into fists.

If he steps closer, I'll remove the smile from his face and take a few teeth with it. Or I'll dig my nails down his cheeks. Rip his face to ribbons.

The voice was small and whispery. Hers, but not hers. Her right hand started to rise, as if it belonged to someone else. She shoved it deep in her pocket. Stepped back.

"Please leave me alone."

He laughed. "Just one drink. Come on."

Kick him where it will hurt, and when he falls—

She moved forward. A half-step, nothing more.

—I'll kick him in the ribs.

What was she thinking? She pushed past one of the smokers, not seeing, not caring. Why had she come here? Behind her, she heard the man's voice, asking her to come back. She quickened her steps and when she approached the corner, she broke into a run. The sensation she'd felt on her skin was nothing more than the wind.

It had to be.

She ran until she reached the front steps of her apartment and stood with her head down, breathing hard. Laughter slipped out from an open window. Genuine, happy laughter, smelling of fresh peaches and newly-bloomed lilacs. It curled like a ribbon around the base of the streetlamp.

When she touched the cold metal, the happiness slipped down, giving her hand plenty of room. She moved her hand. The ribbon moved, too, as if trying to slink away.

No, oh no.

She pulled her hand back and stared at her palms. Saw nothing. But she ran upstairs and took another long shower, scrubbing until the hot water ran to ice. When she finally climbed out, shivering all over, she inspected every inch of her arms, legs, and belly. Using a hand mirror, she checked her back, her neck, her scalp, and sighed in relief.

There was nothing there.

Nothing.

On Monday, the one day when she closed the bookstore, she waited until the morning rush was over and braved the coffee shop on the corner. Traces of frustration and impatience still clung to the ceiling like storm clouds.

She ordered her coffee and took it along with a book, to the park. She planned to read for a few hours until the park became crowded with mothers and their toddlers and their strollers choking up the walkways.

A few pages in, the smell of sour milk wafted by. She closed her book and wrinkled her nose. A homeless man approached her a few moments later.

"Spare some change for a coffee?"

She started to reach in her pocket, then stopped.

The homeless are a menace. They piss on the bushes and pass out on the benches, leaving their filth behind. Someone should take care of the problem. They shouldn't let them in the park at all.

"No, sorry," she said, opening her book again.

"Anything you got will help."

Why won't he just leave me alone?

"I told you, I don't have anything."

"Not even a quarter?"

Her skin exploded with pins and needles. She dropped her book, stood up, and shoved him away. "I said I don't have anything for you. Go away. You stink!"

He staggered back, his toothless mouth in a gaping circle of surprise. "Why'd you do that, lady?"

"I'm sorry, I didn't mean it, I—" She grabbed her book and bolted from the park.

With the shades down, she stood in the middle of the bookstore in a wash of pale half-light, her eyes closed. All around her, she felt the happiness pulling away, withdrawing deep behind the books. Hiding beneath the rug. She touched one of the shelves; the contentment recoiled as if her flesh was laced with toxicity.

A sob broke free.

"Please," she whispered. "Please."

Stop crying. Just stop it.

Meg woke in the middle of the night and padded into the kitchen for a drink of water, wincing at the overhead light. Instead of opening the cabinet, she slid open the silverware drawer, pulled out a knife, and turned it from side to side so the light caught along the edge of the blade.

What would it feel like to slip it beneath someone's skin? Would it be like parting fabric or cutting through overcooked steak? Blood would glimmer on the blade, like ruby pearls. She smiled. The knife was so sharp, it would make it easy. Her limbs flooded with warmth, with possibility.

She thought of the homeless man. Someone like that wouldn't be missed at all. Her hand tightened around the handle. All the breath rushed out of her lungs. She dropped the knife on the floor and stepped back. Away. Those thoughts didn't belong to her.

They didn't.

"I am a good person," she said. "I *am*."

But she could still taste the anticipation on her tongue. Even worse, it wasn't unpleasant. Not in the least.

Beneath the glow of the streetlamps, Meg walked without destination. She crossed street after street, her feet tapping on the pavement. A chill wind blew her hair back from her forehead and stung her cheeks, but she paid it no mind. She walked through the warm pockets that lovers walking hand in hand left behind, ignoring the way the warmth broke apart as she passed.

Strands of happiness drifting on the pavement curled away from her feet.

She held her arms wide, a smile on her face.

Meg woke to the sound of weeping. She sat up, flipped on the bedside light, and cocked her head to the side, but heard only silence. A tear spilled over her lashes and ran down her cheek. Then another. She frowned, wiping them away with the back of her hands.

"Stop it," she said, her voice thick. "Just stop."

While waiting for her tea to cool, Meg sat on her sofa and grabbed the newspaper. The headline on the front page read *Body Found in Cedar Park*. She skimmed the article. Two homeless men had scuffled, over a bench or a bottle, no doubt, and one ended up dead.

"Good riddance."

No, no matter what, he didn't deserve to die, a small insignificant voice whispered deep inside.

She crumpled the newspaper into a ball, threw it on the floor, and grabbed the photo album on her coffee table. She flipped past pictures of her parents in the bookstore, her grandmother's radiant smile, and pictures of herself as a child, many of them showing her with her nose buried in a book.

Pale tendrils the color of daffodils rose from the pages and entwined around her fingers. She frowned. What good were memories? Why had she even bothered to look at the pictures? What a waste of time. She slammed the photo album shut.

No, no! Please.

The tendrils withered to black. Dead stems of useless. She shook off the remnants and trampled them beneath her feet until nothing remained.

Another walk. Another night of solitude and dusk. A car came speeding around a corner, kicking up grime in its wake, and she glared at its taillights.

She crossed the street and stopped. All around her were dilapidated buildings with broken panes of glass and weeds jutting from cracked pavement. She'd walked much further than she'd planned. The air held the bitter taste of hopelessness, and streamers of sorrow hung from the rooftops like tattered clothing.

She smiled.

A shadowy figure stepped into her path, one hand tucked under his jacket. His face too young to wear such menace. Such hunger. Her skin filled with heat.

Need to leave. Need to get away!

"Shut up," she murmured.

"You lost?" he said in a voice roughened at the edges.

"No. Are you?"

Run away. Run now!

He closed the distance between them and grabbed her upper arm with one gloved hand. She straightened her spine. Her smile grew wider. She covered his hand with her own, digging her fingernails in the leather hard, and laughed under her breath.

"What do you want?" she said, stepping close enough to see the pores on his cheeks.

Please, no.

He tried to shake off her hand. His mouth moved; no sound emerged. Her smile stretched again. He took a step back. She took one forward.

He yanked his arm away. Held up one hand. "Look, I don't want any trouble, okay?"

She reached for him again. He shook his head, backed away from her hands, then spun around and took off, his feet heavy on the ground. She laughed into the wind.

No, no, no, this isn't right. This isn't right.

"I said, shut up."

In the dark, beneath the sheets.

Listen to me, please, you have to listen.

Meg rolled over and punched the pillow.

This isn't you, and you know it. You read books to children, you love animals, you give money to the homeless, to charity, you are a good person—

She sat up, clamped her hands over her ears, and shouted, "Shut up, shut up, shut up!"

The voice did.

At eight o'clock on a weeknight, the grocery store was far from crowded. Meg picked up a can of peas, saw a small dent on the side, and set it back on the shelf. A young woman with a toddler came down the opposite end of the aisle, headed in her direction. At least the toddler wasn't screaming.

The woman picked up the dented can of peas and put it in her cart. Not very observant, was she? The toddler knocked another can off the shelf.

"Joey, stop it!"

The woman slapped the child's hand, leaving a small print of red. The toddler burst into tears. So much for not screaming. The baby's hurt, a shocking shade of bright pink, rose through the air and clung to the ceiling tiles, quivering like gelatin and trailing the smell of talcum powder.

"Oh, honey," the woman said, her face a mask of disbelief. "I am sorry. I'm so sorry."

Meg shook her head. If the mother had kept the cart away from the shelf, it wouldn't have happened. She cast a glance back and caught a glimpse of grey on the woman's hand. Just a finger-wide streak that was already fading.

It was my fault. Mine. I touched the can first, and then she did. She never would've struck her child.

That stupid little voice again. What did she know? In private, the mother probably slapped her child at will. Meg pushed her cart out of the aisle with a smile on her face.

Come off.

Meg blinked awake to the stink of bleach. She was sitting on her bathroom floor surrounded with soggy, rust-colored cotton balls, her left arm awash in pain.

"What the…"

She scrambled to her feet. The skin on her arm was bright red, covered with oozing blisters and raw spots flecked with blood. A container of bleach sat open by her feet. This was wrong. She'd been sitting on her sofa, watching television.

No, you can't. I have to—

"You little bitch. How dare you. How did you…"

With her mouth compressed into a thin line, she dumped everything in the trash can and pulled out antibiotic ointment and gauze bandages.

Can't you see what it's doing to you? To me?

"You leave me the hell alone," Meg said.

No, you have to listen. You have to stop this. I know you can. You just have to try. I won't let you do this to me. I won't.

Meg laughed in reply, her fingers curling toward her palms. She'd have to find a way to get rid of the stupid, weak voice once and for all.

Meg stood with the morning crowd on the corner, waiting for the light to change. An elderly woman with frail limbs and fluffy white hair waited next to her, holding tight to a plastic bag. The bag hit Meg in the leg once, twice, three times.

Meg tried to shift away, but the crowd was pressed too close together. The bag hit her again; she bumped into the man on her other side, a man in a cheap suit and a gaudy tie. He gave her a quick look. She gave a frown in return. It was his fault for standing so close. She cast glances over her shoulders. Everyone was watching the street or the light, like cows waiting for the okay to move. No, dumber than cows.

The bag swung against her leg; she bumped into the man. All around, she felt people shifting, a chain reaction of movement and readjustment. The light turned yellow, a collective sigh of relief went up, and the bag hit her again.

"Dammit," she muttered.

And shoved with her shoulder and hip.

No, you can't do this. No!

In a flash, the old woman staggered forward with a shriek. Meg smiled as the bag dropped from the woman's hands and split open on the curb, spilling a dozen dog-eared paperbacks into the street. The old woman's arms pinwheeled, but her upper body was pitched too far forward, and she fell to her hands and knees with a breathy shout. Strands of pale green unfurled from the books like ivy and darted across the asphalt to twine about the woman's ankles. Meg sneered. All the happiness in the world wouldn't save the woman now.

Tires screeched—a car rushing to beat the light. It sped around the woman, and the air filled with the stink of rubber on asphalt.

What have you done?

Someone edged closer to Meg, brushed up against her shoulder, and a second later, laughed. A soft laugh mostly under the breath. And then another from elsewhere in the crowd. And another.

"Stupid old bag," someone hissed.

No, I will not let you do this. I will not.

The smell of char hung heavy in the air, thick and malevolent. The laughter grew louder. All around her, strands of grey curled out, over, around, the people.

Please, please help me.

The green uncurled from the woman's ankles and moved toward Meg. More ribbons slipped down from streetlamps and doors and danced in waves across the street. All heading in the same direction.

Meg squirmed, but she couldn't break free from the crowd. Laughter rose overhead in dark bubbles glistening with a fiery shade of red. A thin tendril of green made its way over the curb and touched the tip of Meg's foot.

Yes, please help me.

"Get away, get away from me," she said, twisting her body this way and that.

The man in the suit bumped into Meg, hard enough to knock her sideways several inches. Her hands came up instinctively, hands caked with grey, like overlapping scales, each one glistening as if dipped in a slick of oil. All across her arms, more of the same.

This is not who you are, the voice said.

The ribbon of green wound its way up around her leg.

No, you will not do this.

Meg extended her arms, fingers splayed. Streamers of pink, yellow, and lilac rushed along the pavement, darting between feet and legs, all on a path to Meg. They spiraled around her calves, coiled about her waist, and danced along her arms, nudging their way beneath the grey.

Cracks appeared in her arms with zigzags of healthy flesh peeking out. The air filled with the smell of hibiscus and rose. The corners of her mouth slid up into a smile as she tasted strength and purpose—

No, it was weakness. Useless, stupid weakness. They would not win. She would not *let* them win.

In the street, the elderly woman rose to her feet. Tires screeched again. Another car swerved, but the tires didn't catch on the asphalt. The car slid in an arc, the side heading straight for

the woman, close enough for Meg to see the driver's mouth open
in a giant O. The laughter of the crowd grew louder.

The grey pressed back, tightening around Meg's limbs. One
green tendril dropped to the pavement, the severed edge bleeding
pale vapor onto the pavement. Her laughter

No, not mine, not mine.

joined the rest.

The ribbons wrapped even tighter around her limbs, propelling
her forward, as if she were a marionette and they the puppeteer. She
struggled and pushed, but couldn't stop, couldn't break free.

This is who you really are.

They shoved her through the crowd, out into the street, and let
go. She fell against the old woman, pushing her out of the way to
safety. Someone laughed; in the distance, someone else screamed.

Metal met flesh as the car struck.

Pain exploded inside Meg's chest, her back, her legs. She felt
the sensation of flying, then a thud as she landed on her back.
Hurt came anew. Everywhere. Inside and out. She stared at the
sky, a seeping warmth crept from beneath her body, and the taste
of wet pennies filled her mouth.

She tried to move her legs, but the signal would not pass between brain and limb. Tried to speak, but the words would not come.
Like a broken, discarded doll, she remained motionless and still.

With a soft tug, the grey left her skin. A legion of rats desert-
ing their sinking ship. A dark shadow moved across the asphalt,
and the smell of char rose into the air. Sirens wailed far in the distance. Too late. They were too late. Tears filled Meg's eyes.

Green and yellow and pink took the grey's place, wrapping
around her like streamers on a Maypole. She tasted the sweetness
of honeysuckle; the pain ebbed; the sirens faded to a mere suggestion of sound.

This is who you are, the voice whispered, soft and sweet. *This is
who you are.*

Girl,
With Coin

❧ ❧

The girl who can't feel pain is on display in the art gallery again.

Stitches bind her lips together, a cage to keep her voice prisoner. The seams of her costume feel as if they'll split under the strain of holding herself in.

She stares into the crowd with her back straight. In her hand, she clutches a straight razor, the blade glittering under the lights like a dark promise of blood, a pulse slowing to nothing at all.

She doesn't have a death wish. She isn't suicidal. Suicide isn't art. It's cheap theater, not even off-Broadway quality. Anyone can do it.

And she isn't into kink. Her show isn't designed to get anyone off. It's about how much you can stand before you say enough, before you break.

Before you turn away.

Title: A Study in Crucifixion
Medium: Specially cast nails patterned after those used in ancient Rome
Canvas: Wrists, feet

Olivia steps on the envelope as she's heading out of her apartment. If not for the crinkle of paper, she might not have even noticed. It's plain white with the sealed side facing up. When she sees her name scrawled across the front in familiar handwriting with a distinctive O, the breath rushes out of her and her fingers tremble.

She scans the hallway but she's alone except for the smell of burnt toast from the neighbors. Holding the letter as if it contains something toxic, she carries it back inside, kicks the door shut behind her.

The last time she saw that O, it was scrawled across a paper lunch bag. She was thirteen, her left leg encased in a cast up to her thigh, her left arm a series of scrapes and bruises, her ribs taped. Damage on display for everyone for see.

She contemplates throwing the envelope away unopened (she's meeting Trevor for coffee and doesn't want to be late) but leans against the door and slides her finger beneath the flap. No paper cut, no hint of red, but the letter hurts anyway with its very presence. It hurts deep inside where the bruises and scars don't show. That's the worst part. She should've put it behind her, moved on.

The envelope holds a single piece of paper, folded in uneven creases. She frowns. Was she not even worth the effort of making it neat? She taps the letter against her palm. Unfolding it will mean ending twelve years of silence. She exhales. Unfolds the paper.

I'm sure you don't want to hear from me after all this time.

Olivia closes her eyes, thumps her head on the door. Her fingers seek the scar just above her heart. Once upon a time, it was faint, but she's reopened it so many times (the way you open a favorite book—not for the purpose of art), now the scar is thick and ridged, easy to find even beneath the fabric of her shirt.

The rest of the letter is short: *I know it's been a long time but I'd love to talk to you. Maybe we could meet for coffee or you could just call me. I hope you don't hate me too much. There's so much I want and need to explain.*

Thankfully, she didn't sign it Mom, but with her first name— Marie. There's a phone number, a local number. What's missing is an apology. Surely Marie could've summoned up enough humility, even bullshit humility, for that. Olivia traces the scar on her chest again, then crumples the letter in a tight ball.

She remembers her mother sitting in the kitchen with the overhead light turned off and the small room awash in shadows. Olivia watched, hidden behind a half-open door, as her mother tossed a coin in the air. She let it sit on her palm for a long time before she closed her fingers. When Olivia woke the next morning, her mother was gone, but she left the coin, a quarter minted in the year of Olivia's birth, on the kitchen table. A final act of cruelty, a strange coincidence, or the perceived worth of her daughter's life?

Olivia's chest tightens. *Maybe,* she thinks, *parts of you never move on, away, no matter how much you want them to.* Then again, her inability to feel pain affects her body's ability to heal. Maybe it has the same effect on her heart.

"Fuck you," she whispers.

She carries the letter outside and tosses it in the first trash can she passes. She chain smokes her way to the café and pretends the catch in her throat is from the harsh tobacco.

Title: Roses in Bloom
Medium: Wild roses, with thorns, on the vine, wire wrapping
Canvas: Entire body

Olivia watches Trevor's face as he looks over her sketch. He's chewing the inside of his cheek, as always, a habit she's glad she doesn't have. She wouldn't know when to stop and walking around with a hole in her face would be unpleasant; it would turn her from artist into freakshow. While she waits, she rubs a scar on the back of her hand, the last remaining trace of her last exhibit. The scar is bright pink against the pale of her skin, but soon enough it will fade to match the rest of them. Her hands heal slower than anything else.

She reaches for her coffee cup but hesitates and rests her hand on the edge of the table instead. She can't tell from Trevor's expression what he's thinking, but she's afraid she knows the answer. It's too much. It's too in your face.

Why did she contact me?

Finally, he slides the sketch back across the table and nods his head. "I like it. I like it a lot. It really pushes the envelope."

She lets out a breath. "You don't think it's too…extreme?"

"No, I think people will love it. Some might freak out, but whatever. Anyone who's been to one of your shows will know what to expect."

She slides her coffee over. "Is this safe for me to drink yet?"

He takes a sip and nods. "Yeah, it's good."

(The tasting is a minor inconvenience. Far better than the helmet her father insisted she wear as a young child to keep from giving herself a concussion or worse, even when playing alone in her room. At least once she started school, he allowed her to leave the helmet at home.)

Why in the hell did she contact me?

Many people mistakenly think she can't feel anything, but she feels textures, hunger, the pressure of an embrace, the pleasure of an orgasm. Only her pain receptors are screwed up. The condition itself is rare and has a pretty medical term, but she prefers to call it genetic fuckery.

She cups the mug in her hands. The ceramic is warm to the touch, but it could be scorching hot and she wouldn't know. Since she can't sense extremes in temperatures, she has to check the weather each day so she knows how to dress. "Anything you want changed?" She peeks at her hands; her skin isn't bright red.

"No, not at all. I'll get everything squared away on my end. And you're okay with the fifteenth? I'd give you the Saturday before but I've got the contortionists coming in again."

"The fifteenth is fine."

"Excellent. I'll print up flyers."

It's her turn to nod, and as she does, she traces her finger over the title of the sketch: *Yesterday's Girl.*

"Are you okay?"

"Of course. Why?"

"You seem, I don't know, on edge."

"No," she says, putting on a smile that feels too small, too tight. "I'm fine."

On her way home, Olivia hits a vintage shop filled with odds and ends in various condition. She doesn't find any useful clothing. Sure, she could go online and order something in pinup girl style, but she doesn't want anything made in the now. The prices are crazy high for what she requires, and she wants the wear, the frayed edges, the split seams.

In a display case in the back, she finds a straight razor with a mother of pearl handle. Perfect. There's a bit of rust on the razor's blade, but no nicks or dings, and she knows it will sharpen nicely.

She presses the tip against her finger and keeps pressing until her skin opens. The small cut won't take long to heal at all. She turns and there's a salesgirl standing with wide eyes, one hand over her mouth.

"Don't worry," Olivia says. "I had a tetanus shot last year."

But she recognizes the look all too well. If she were within the walls of the gallery, she'd revel in it, and even though she shoves her hand in her pocket, hiding the cut, she has to fight not to press the blade against her skin again.

Title: Stigmata in Repose
Medium: Whip, knife, skewer
Canvas: Palms, feet, back, forehead, side

When the moon is full in the sky, Olivia takes a paring knife from her nightstand. This blade will never be part of her exhibits; it's hers and hers alone, a token from her childhood. She opens the scar on her chest and watches as the blood trickles down. Would her mother remember this? She had to, didn't she? Or would it be another afterthought, a horror, like her daughter?

As a child, blood was a sign of danger: scratches on a cheek from a too long fingernail; glass in the ball of a bare foot; teeth accidentally biting through lips and tongue. Every family photo album was a symphony of wounds—major breaks and minor stitches. Now, blood is only a sign of possibility, of how far she can push herself.

She threw out the albums after her father died. They were reminders she neither needed nor wanted. It was obvious, once you looked past the casts and the bandages, that her mother never stood close to Olivia in any of the photos. Her smile was always strained, her eyes distant. She couldn't even fake it well.

Olivia wipes the blood from her chest, and the realization that her mother knows where she lives sinks in. She can't imagine her mother would knock on the door and invite herself in, but it leaves Olivia with an uneasy feeling in her gut.

Title: The Human Pincushion (Inspired by the movie Hellraiser)
Medium: Small sewing pins
Canvas: Entire body, including shaved head

She finds the right outfit in another vintage shop on the other side of town. It costs more than she wanted to spend, but it's perfect. It's a swimming costume, not a bathing suit, all sequins and ribbons with a short, ruffled skirt, and she bets the woman who owned it never set foot in ocean or pool. The fabric holds a ghost of perfume beneath the scent of old fabric. It isn't an exact fit, but with a few nips and tucks, it will be. In the dressing room mirror, she stares at herself for a long time, the scars on her body a patch-work of intersecting lines, tiny road maps leading nowhere.

The delicate designs of a puzzle box hiding a monster, but unlike a Cenobite, the sensory overload of her ritual mutilation will never come.

Halfway home, she feels the weight of unseen eyes on her. She stops on the sidewalk. All around her are shops and people walking. No one looks familiar; no one is paying her any atten-tion. Still, she cannot shake the feeling that someone is watching.

Title: Why Don't You Love Me?
Medium: Paring Knife
Canvas: Chest, directly above the heart

A second letter arrives via the regular mail with a local postmark. She throws it out unread.

Title: The Ghost at the Table
Medium: Salad fork
Canvas: Arms

Olivia wakes in the middle of the night with traces of a dream still playing through her mind—her mother's face, the shiny blade of the knife, the blood on skin and silver. She sits up in bed and lights a cigarette. Blows smoke into the air. Finally, she gets up and starts sketching ideas for the next exhibit, but every idea be-comes a crumple of paper littering the floor.

Then, she sketches a woman with the skin of her chest peeled to expose her ribcage and the heart beneath. She writes *Changeling* across the top of the paper. It's something she overheard her mother say once, along with freak and monster. Did she know Olivia was listening?

Olivia smiles, small and hard. She supposes she *was* hard to endure. It's not as if there were manuals on what to do when your teething child chewed off the tip of her pinkie, and the disorder was too rare for any sort of support group.

She slides her finger over the sketch. It's an impossible design. She might as well call herself Kafka's darling and wither away in a cage, forgotten by all. Fuck that.

Title: Attention Lure
Medium: Fish hooks
Canvas: Arms

The week before the exhibit, she sharpens the razor and replenishes her first aid kit. She has surgical glue, bandages, thread, a curved needle. A prescription for antibiotics is filled and ready to go, and she's been taking extra iron. The alterations to the bathing costume are complete, the poses practiced and practiced again. There isn't anything else she needs to do but the performance itself.

Another letter arrives two days before the exhibit. She burns it in her ashtray.

Title: Shake, Rattle, and Buzz
Medium: Beehive
Canvas: Arms, legs, face

At what point did she decide her mother's horror and revulsion were emotions to be desired? Invoked? Was it the derogatory names she heard whispered? The refusal to touch her? Perhaps the young Olivia thought it a game: *Look what I can do, Mommy.*

But what good is a slap if a small face turns red but the mouth doesn't twist and the eyes don't fill with tears? What help is a boundary if crossing it carries no fear? What price do you pay when a coin means nothing more than goodbye?

At the age of thirteen, when Olivia stepped into the street, she knew the car was moving too slowly to kill her. After the impact, when she was on the ground with a bone protruding from her calf like an exclamation point, she watched her mother's face, certain this time would be different. This time her mother would pretend to care.

Her mother remained expressionless, her eyes blank.

Two nights later, Olivia went into the living room and slid the paring knife across her chest. Her skin split like delicate silk, spilling out a crimson worm.

Look what I can do, Mommy.

Her mother didn't even blink.

Maybe Olivia should have cut deeper and pulled out her heart. Held it in her palm while the beats counted down to nothing. Maybe that would've made her mother happy. *See? I was real after all.*

A week later, Olivia watched her flip the coin and make her choice.

Title: Toddler Interrupted
Medium: Shards of glass
Canvas: Soles of feet, fingers

The gallery is packed, everyone standing shoulder to shoulder. Olivia stands before them on a small raised platform, the base covered with white butcher paper, her mouth sewn shut with heavy black thread. She makes a few poses of the cheesy, pinup girl variety and is rewarded with a titter of laughter. Faces show confusion, but that's to be expected. There's no blood yet, and her other exhibits have been static.

She lifts the straight razor, cuts through the stitches, careful *not* to draw blood. Brows crease, mouths twist, whispers emerge.

Her lipstick becomes a smear across one side of her face with the back of a hand. She twists her fingers in the careful rolls of her hair, pulls them out of shape and keeps pulling until they're a tangle. She tears one of the straps of her costume, and sequins fall like iridescent fish scales.

She gives the crowd a wide smile as she draws the blade across her forearm. Several people gasp. The wound curves, another smile, and the red it reveals matches her lipstick. Drops of blood patter on the butcher paper. She knows how to wield the blade for maximum effect with minimal damage.

She watches their eyes. Even when their mouths twist in revulsion or disbelief, their eyes reveal the truth. A glint here, a shimmer there. Hunger. They're waiting for her to slip and open a vein. They come for the shock factor, but it's not what they really want to see. They're vultures, waiting for her to fall so they can pick at her bones.

For several long moments, the red dripping down onto the white is the only sound. Then someone exhales loudly. A grey-haired woman in the front holds her mouth tight, but she can't lie away the excitement in her eyes. Olivia meets her gaze, and the woman looks down. Another woman, younger, with flushed cheeks, covers her mouth with a hand.

Olivia switches the blade to the other hand and slices a twin cut on her other arm. Two more cuts and she can hear whispers, voices too low to decipher into words.

A man in a suit shoves his hands in his pockets, his eyes revealing disbelief, perhaps a touch of disappointment at Olivia's lack of response. She's a sadist's worst nightmare.

None of the reactions surprise her. At this point they're a guarantee, made mundane by their predictability. What she notices most are the empty eyes. The blank canvases that say nothing. She'd like to chip away their façades and peek inside. She'd like to break them into pieces.

She makes another cut, then she sees the woman standing in the back. Twelve years have added grey to the hair and lines around the eyes and mouth, but the face is immediately recognizable and far too like Olivia's own for her liking.

Olivia makes another cut and another, until her arms look like railroad tracks. Her mother doesn't blink, doesn't move. All the years she watched Olivia, she never did a damn thing. Somewhere inside Olivia there is a little girl who wants to throw down the razor and scream, who wants to know why. Why didn't her mother understand why Olivia did the things she did? Why didn't she know that all Olivia wanted was one reaction, one fucking reaction, to let her know she cared?

Why didn't her mother stop her?

Olivia clenches her jaw, tugs her top aside to reveal the scar on her chest, and draws the razor down to reopen the half-healed wound. From the gap, she wiggles a quarter free, breaking the tenuous grip her flesh has on the metal. She turns it so the lights reveal the tarnish of time beneath the slick of blood.

The crowd doesn't understand the significance, nor do they need to. It's another macabre parlor trick and gauging by their smiles, one they like. But her mother's face pales and, finally, she breaks free from the crowd and heads out the door without a glance over her shoulder. Olivia's own shoulders sag, and something inside her crumples, like a paper cup beneath a boot heel.

A woman near the front sways. Silence shatters into murmurs of concern, a bit of laughter from the unbalanced woman. Olivia curls her fist around the coin and gives a small nod.

Yesterday's Girl is over.

When the applause fades and almost everyone is gone, she plucks the ends of thread from her lips and wipes away the lipstick smears. Some of the blood has already dried on her skin, but instead of cleaning and disinfecting the cuts, she wraps her arms in gauze, shrugs on a jacket and jeans over her costume, and slips out before Trevor notices. She knows he'll be upset; they usually get something to eat after an exhibit, but she doesn't have the heart for it. Not tonight.

Across the street, she sees a figure standing beneath the yellow glow of a streetlamp. Olivia pulls the quarter from her pocket and bounces it on her palm. Such a small, insignificant thing. Such a heavy price.

Heads, she'll cross the street. Perhaps they can have coffee at a diner. Maybe her mother will finally tell her why.

Tails, she'll head home. Sketch a new exhibit, something less extreme. Let the cut on her chest heal for good this time, throw the quarter in a fountain, a gutter. Give herself permission to let everything go.

She stares into the shadows for a long time, waiting, hoping her mother will walk away, but she doesn't. She stands and waits.

Olivia touches the cut above her heart and flips the coin.

Paskutinis Iliuzija
(The Last Illusion)

 ❧ ❧

Andrius Kavalauskas, the last magician of Lithuania, closed the door and rested his head against the wood as the nurse's footsteps faded away. He smelled cabbage and pork cooking from the apartment across the hallway and knew that in a few hours he would find a plate of food sitting by his door. Daina was a good neighbor, a good friend.

He headed back into the tiny bedroom at the back of the apartment. Laurita was a still and silent shape beneath the threadbare blanket. Far too still.

He froze in place. Stared at the blanket. Heard neither breath nor whisper. *No, no. Not yet. Please, not yet*, he thought.

Then, the blanket moved up and down. Laurita raised her head and smiled. He exhaled, the sound harsh in the quiet.

"Papa, was I a good girl for the nurse?"

"Of course you were. Miss Ruta said you were *very* good."

"She had a sad face. I thought…"

"No, no, you are always a good girl. Always."

"When I feel better, I should pick flowers for her. Would that be okay?"

Andrius's chest tightened. For a moment, the words caught in his throat. He nodded. "Yes, it would be very nice."

Outside the window, storm clouds gathered and thunder rumbled in the distance.

"Is Perkūnas angry?" Laurita asked.

He laughed. "Maybe he is."

She gave him a small smile. "Papa?"

"Yes?"

"Who makes the snow?"

He tapped his chin. "I wonder. Is it Perkūnas?"

She shook her head. "No, he makes the thunder."

"Jūratė?"

Another shake. A small giggle. "No, she lives in the sea."

"Ahhhh, I know," he said, raising his hand. In his palm, a white ball of snow shimmered in the light. "*I* make the snow!" He tossed it up in the air. It broke apart, and snowflakes fell down around her, alighting on her lashes and nose. The room filled with the smell of pine and cinnamon.

She gave a weak laugh, her breath emerging in a vapory plume. As the snowflakes melted, he could not help looking over both shoulders. No one could possibly have felt such a small magic, and the curtains were shut tight, but still...

"You have the best magic in the world," Laurita said.

He kissed her forehead. "I have the best daughter in the world, but now, you must go to sleep."

"Okay," she said, her eyes already half-closed.

He pretended not to notice the pale cast to her skin. The shadows beneath her eyes. Her frail limbs. The breath wheezing in and out of her lungs. Just as he pretended not to see the soldiers outside. It was

safer

better that way.

Andrius tossed and turned in his own bed, hating the way the space beside him felt like a country he could only dream of visiting. Wind rattled against the glass, and a boom sounded in the distance. Maybe Perkūnas was wielding the bolts of thunder and lightning. Maybe not. He was also the god of war, yet he seemed in no hurry to strike down the invaders. Perhaps he didn't care at all.

The rest of the world was far too busy watching Paris fall to the Germans to worry about Andrius's country and the suffering of its people. There were whispers of ways out, of soldiers who would look the other way for the right amount of money, but he did not have the money, and Laurita was not strong enough for travel.

He scrubbed his face with his hands. A trace of magic lingered on his skin, giving his palm a luminescent appearance. Such a small thing. Such a huge risk. But it was all he had.

Saulė had always loved the snowflakes, too.

He rolled over to the empty side of the bed and buried his face in her pillow. He could still smell the scent of her skin. Tears burned in his eyes. He inhaled deeply, pulling in her scent as far as he could.

She would still be with them if he hadn't let her go out on her own. He'd known it was dangerous. But she'd smiled and said she'd be right back, she was only going to the market, and he'd kissed her on the cheek and said, "Okay." He should've said no, it was not okay. He was supposed to protect her.

He punched the mattress and sobbed into the pillow. It was all his fault and there was nothing he could do. He could only pray they took her to Siberia. At least there she would have a chance. A tiny one, but better than the alternative.

"Oh, Saulė, I miss you. I miss you so much," he said, his voice muffled. "Please forgive me."

He should've done something. *Anything.* He cried until his throat ached, then clasped his hands together and prayed. He prayed Ruta made it home safe and sound. He prayed for his country. He prayed for Saulė. And last, he prayed for a miracle for Laurita. He wished with all his heart she would see her seventh birthday. Surely the gods could grant him that.

Coughing woke him in the middle of the night. He stumbled in the darkness, banging his shin on the doorframe. Laurita was hunched over in the bed, her hands cupped over her mouth. The coughs came out ragged and thick. He rubbed her back and held a cloth to her mouth until the coughing subsided.

After he wiped the blood from her lips, he tucked the cloth away before she could see it and measured out a spoonful of the medicine Ruta, his wife's best friend in the time before fear and soldiers, had risked her life to bring. It was not a curative (those medicines belonged to other countries, countries without soldiers and tanks invading their lands) but would make it…easier for her.

Laurita made a face. "I don't like medicine."

"I don't either." He smiled. "Here, let's make it taste better." He waved his hand. The liquid turned amber; the sweet smell of

flowers wafted from the spoon. She swallowed it down and
smiled.

"Will the medicine help me get better?"

"Yes, it will."

"And when I am well, will Mama come back?"

He swallowed hard and forced his lips into a smile. "I'm sure
she will finish her work and come home soon."

A little lie. Just like the taste of honey in her spoon.

"I wish the soldiers could find someone else to help them. I
miss her, Papa. I miss her so much."

"I miss her, too."

"Magic me a story, Papa."

"I wish I could, but you know it would make the soldiers angry. I will tell you a story instead."

"Okay."

"And what story do you want to hear?"

Her face brightened. "Jūratė and Kastytis."

He smiled. Saulė had told her the story time and again. He
always thought it too sad for a small child, but it was Laurita's
favorite. He readjusted the curtains, fluffed Laurita's pillow, and
pulled the blanket up to her chin.

"Once upon a time, there was a beautiful mermaid goddess
who lived under the sea in a palace made of amber. Her name was
Jūratė, and she had a long tail with scales the color of the sky just
before the sun sets.

"And there was a handsome fisherman named Kastytis who
would come to the sea every day to catch fish, but one day, while
Kastytis was in his boat, Perkūnas was angry and made a big
storm."

Andrius let a little magic slip free. Just a touch of the salt tang
of the Baltic Sea and a darkening of the air near the ceiling to re-
semble a storm cloud.

"Kastytis fell into the sea. Jūratė saw him fall and rescued him
from the waves. She took him home to her palace, and they fell in
love.

"But this made Perkūnas very angry. He didn't think Jūratė
should love a mortal man like Kastytis. He wanted her to marry
Patrimpas, the God of Water. In his anger, he sent a lightning bolt
from the sky through the water."

Andrius made light flash in the air, one quick snap of soundless bright.

"The lightning hit Jūratė's palace, shattering it into thousands and thousands of fragments, and poor Kastytis was killed.

"Perkūnas punished Jūratė by chaining her to the ruins of her castle. And now, when storms strike the sea, you can hear Jūratė crying for Kastytis, and you can find her tears washed upon the shore."

He held out his hand and opened his fingers, revealing a tiny piece of amber that Laurita took and held up to the light. It glowed with a secret fire, then it winked out of sight. She put her hand down and looked at him for a long time without speaking, her mouth set into a frown, her eyes filled with a seriousness far too advanced for her years.

"Perkūnas should have not made the storm and the thunder. He should've protected the palace instead, and he should've left Jūratė and Kastytis alone."

"It's just a story, little one. Only a story."

But the frown did not leave her face.

"Papa, why does the magic make the soldiers angry?"

"I don't know," he lied.

From his bedroom window, Andrius could see the edge of a striped awning at the end of the street. A theater, its stage now silent and dark. He'd performed there a long time ago, but he still remembered the heat of the lights and the gasps of surprise from the audience.

The best magicians could make the people forget they were seated indoors, could transport them to another time, another place. Lithuanian magic was no mere sleight of hand or game of misdirection, but a gift from the land, born from the spring breeze and the winter chill, the fir tree and the rivers.

It could create lions from shadows and birds from candleflame. Could send snowfall on a summer day and turn tears into rain. Even if you were not in a theater during a performance, you could stand outside and feel it in the air, a silent music pulsing from the magician's fingertips. It was power, but not of control or destruction. It gave hope. Happiness. Strength. All the things the Russians wanted to take away.

Saulė had not wanted him to stop performing, but life on the stage belonged to a man without responsibilities. He'd traded the theater for small magics to make her smile and later, to calm their infant daughter. A choice he never regretted.

And if he had he not made that choice… He closed his eyes. He'd heard whispers that even the old magicians who'd lost their magic to disease or dementia had disappeared.

How he had escaped notice, he didn't know.

"I don't want to eat, Papa."

Andrius set the bowl down and smoothed her hair back from her forehead. "But you must. You need your strength."

She shook her head. "I will eat it later."

"But the rabbit might eat it first."

"The rabbit?"

"Yes, the rabbit."

He cupped his hands together, blew into them, and opened his palms to reveal a tiny brown rabbit, its nose wiggling, its ears twitching. He placed the rabbit on the bed. It hopped once, twice, three times, and Laurita giggled and clapped her hands.

"Can we keep him?"

"Only for a little while," he whispered.

He guided the rabbit over to Laurita's bowl. It dipped its head in.

"No, rabbit, that's my food."

"Okay, you eat it then."

She took several spoonfuls, watching the rabbit jump around on her bed. When the soup was gone, the rabbit turned translucent, shimmering at the edges. Then it disappeared.

"Can you bring it back?"

"No, it's too dangerous. I will tell you a story instead.

"Once upon a time, the Grand Duke Gediminas went on a hunting trip and made camp atop a high mountain. That night, he dreamt of an iron wolf on the mountain. The wolf howled and howled and howled and sounded like hundreds of wolves.

"When he woke, he told the priest of his dream. The priest said it meant that Gediminas was to build a city on the mountain. The city would be as strong as iron and stand tall for hundreds of years.

"Gediminas had his castle built, and it still stands today, here in Vilnius."

He held out his hand. On his palm rested a miniature version of the circular castle, the striped flag of Lithuania flying strong and proud.

"I think you would build a better castle, Papa. A bigger, stronger one to keep everyone safe."

Andrius bent over the bed to adjust the blankets. "Everything will work out fine, little one. I'm sure of it."

He hoped his voice sounded convincing.

Andrius was sleeping in a chair in the front room when footsteps thudded in the hall. Coarse voices spoke in Russian. He sprang up from the chair and ran into Laurita's bedroom. She was sleeping soundly. He closed her bedroom door, his mouth dry, his palms sweaty.

His hands twisted. Maybe the soldiers would not check the rest of the apartment. He stood up straight, took a deep breath, and waited three feet away from the door.

Someone shouted. A soldier laughed. A woman screamed. He covered his mouth with his hand and cast a gaze toward Laurita's door.

Please let her sleep through it, he thought.

More footsteps. Closer now.

Prašau, prašau.

He dropped his hands at his side. He would not let them see that he was afraid. A thump. Another laugh. A sob. A child's cries.

Prašau.

Then the footsteps led away. *Away.* His shoulders sagged. He could not hold in his tears.

"Ačiū Dievo," he whispered.

They were safe. This time.

"Papa?"

He rushed into the bedroom.

"I heard voices."

"It was just the neighbors. That's all. Go back to sleep now. Everything is fine."

"Okay."

He sagged against the doorframe. No more magic. It was too dangerous. And what good was it? All the magic in the world couldn't make her well again.

A soft knock sounded at the door just after the sun rose. Andrius opened it a crack, saw Daina standing in the hall, and ushered her in.

"They took Gedrius and his whole family," she whispered. "But I saw one of them visit Raimondas's apartment after they took them away."

"Raimondas? No, he wouldn't do something like that. He wouldn't. He is a good man."

"He is a scared man, like all of us, and scared men do foolish things sometimes." She touched his arm. "You must be careful."

Andrius raked his fingers through his hair. "I am careful"

She took his hands and gave them a small shake. "No, you need to be *careful*. Do you understand?"

"Yes."

"Good."

A sick feeling twisted inside his belly. "If something should happen to me, will you..." He cleared his throat. "Will you care for Laurita?"

She nodded slowly. "I will do what I can."

After she left, he stood in the doorway to Laurita's bedroom and watched her sleep. Her breath was too shallow, the movement of her chest, too slight. Tears ran down his cheeks.

Daina must be mistaken. Raimondas would not turn anyone in. Maybe it was just coincidence. Gedrius's wife had been a pretty woman. The soldiers liked pretty women. He shuddered.

He should have made Saulė stay home. She had been beautiful.

Once, the small apartment had smelled of flowers, of Saulė's perfume. Of hope. Now, only the scent of illness hung in the air. Andrius opened his hand, and wisps of pale pink floated up. The smell of freshly-cut roses danced in the air, but it was only a poor imitation. He closed his fist tight, and the scent vanished as if it had never been there at all.

Through a gap in the curtains, he saw a group of soldiers sauntering down the street, their boots trailing mud on the cobblestones. A small boy darted out of another apartment building. One of the soldiers grabbed his arm, and the rest laughed.

Andrius raised his fist to bang on the glass, but pulled it back before it struck. He turned away. The boy's high-pitched cries crept into the apartment. Andrius covered his ears and rocked back and forth. The boy was so small. So small. Andrius wanted to help, but he couldn't. He *couldn't*. The cries went on and on.

Eventually they stopped, and the soldiers marched on. Andrius dared another look, but the boy was nowhere to be seen.

Laurita was fast asleep, even though the sun was only beginning to set. She'd refused to eat anything all day, claiming her stomach hurt. He kissed her forehead, went into his own bedroom, and pretended to sleep.

"Please, Laurita, you must eat."

"But I'm not hungry now. Can I eat later? Please?"

He nodded. "Okay. Later."

She coughed softly. Once. Twice. The cough became loud and liquid and thick. He sat her up and held a cloth to her mouth while he rubbed her back. Her body shook with the force of each cough.

Finally, it subsided enough for a spoonful of medicine. She grimaced, but swallowed it without complaint. He held her close, listening to the air rattle in her lungs. Smelled the coppery tinge of her breath.

I am sorry, Saulė, I did the best I could.

It wasn't enough. Not nearly enough.

"Papa, will I be well soon?"

"Yes, very soon."

"Good. I am tired of being sick. I want to pick flowers."

She coughed again, weakly. Her skin was cool and clammy. He pressed a finger to her wrist; her pulse raced beneath, thready and inconsistent. Tears blurred his vision. He blinked them away and shoved his sorrow deep inside.

"Papa?"

"Yes?"

"I wish the soldiers would let Mama come back for a little while so I could tell her I love her."

His tears returned. This time, he turned his head and wiped his eyes dry.

"She knows you love her. I promise."

"But I want to tell her. It's not fair."

"No, it isn't fair. I wish they would let her come home, too." He sighed and looked down at his hands. None of it was fair. "But they told me I could magic you a story."

"They did?"

"Yes, just this one time, it was okay."

She struggled up to a sitting position. He rearranged the pillow behind her. His hands shook, but he touched her cheek. He had failed in so many ways. As a husband. As a father. As a man. He could give his daughter this much. It would not make up for what he didn't do, nothing could do that, but it was the only gift he knew how to give.

No matter the risk to himself.

"Once upon a time, there was a beautiful mermaid goddess who lived under the sea in a palace made of amber."

He lifted his hand and swept it through the air. The walls of the bedroom glistened and turned sapphire blue in color. Ripples moved in lazy lines up and down. At the edges, where ceiling met wall and wall met floor, white foam gathered. The distant cry of seabirds drifted in the air. The room filled with the scent of the sea.

A tiny shimmering light began to glow. It grew larger and larger, revealing a palace with gilded spires.

"It's beautiful," Laurita whispered.

Multicolored fish swam in and out of the palace's many windows. Then Jūratė swam out of the front entrance, her dark hair flowing in the water. Her tail was covered with purple-blue scales, her fins tipped with gold. Laurita's eyes widened.

Andrius waved his hand again. The air around them changed color. First aquamarine, then sapphire, rippling around them in slow, gentle waves, and through the water above their heads, a man's face became visible. A young, handsome man holding a fishing rod in one hand and a fish in the other.

Jūratė swam closer to the surface. Kastytis leaned forward; his mouth formed a circle, and he fell into the water with a splash. Droplets landed on Laurita's brow. Andrius wiped them away.

Jūratė pulled Kastytis into her arms, and they spun around in the water. Tiny pink and yellow fish circled them, moving fast enough to create the illusion of ribbons.

Laurita smiled. "They are so happy."

Then a man with stormy eyes looked down through the water, his mouth set into a frown. In his hand, he held a bolt of lightning. He raised his arm.

"Papa, don't let him destroy the castle. Please!"

"But that's how the story goes."

"No, you can change the story, can't you?"

Andrius sucked in a breath. He gave his tears to the sea and tried to find a smile, but inside, his heart clenched tight. He nodded.

No matter the risk.

The magic stretched within him, filling his limbs with strength. He pushed it out, farther than he'd allowed in years. It made Laurita's skin shine, stripping the pallor of grey. She laughed, high and crystal clear.

The water rippled again. Perkūnas's frown disappeared into a smile. The amber palace gleamed. A fish swam close, its scales a brilliant crimson, and Laurita reached out to touch its fin. It swam back around and let her touch it again. Jūratė let go of Kastytis and swam over to the bed, offered Laurita a smile and her hand.

"Papa, is it okay?"

"Yes, I think it is."

The magic grew and grew. Jūratė took Andrius's hand as well and tugged them down into the water, toward the castle.

"Can we go in?" Laurita whispered.

Jūratė nodded. She swam between them as they walked up the amber steps into a room with an arched ceiling. The floor was a circular mosaic of amber in varying shades. The walls, thin sheets of amber the color of honey fresh from the comb.

"Papa, it's the most beautiful thing ever."

Footsteps thumped in the hall, and his heartbeat quickened.

Not yet. Please, not yet.

"I love you, my princess."

Voices rose in anger. Andrius looked over his shoulder. Through the magic, he could just make out the bedroom door.

"Papa?"

"Everything is okay," he said, forcing his voice to remain steady.

"Is it the soldiers?"

"Yes."

"But they said you could magic me a story, and it's not finished yet."

"I guess they changed their minds. I think they need me to go work with them for a little while."

Jūratė let go of Andrius's hand, but kept Laurita's.

Andrius bent down in front of Laurita and brushed her hair back from her face. "But while I go and work with the soldiers, how would you like to stay here?"

"Could I?"

He looked up at Jūratė. She nodded.

"See?"

"You won't be gone a long time like Mama, will you?"

Jūratė leaned close, her voice soft and whispery like sea foam. "I will keep her safe."

A fist banged on the door. He wrapped his arms around Laurita and kissed her cheeks.

"I don't want you to go," she said, her eyes filled with tears.

"I have to, my sweet girl, I have to, but I will see you soon. I promise."

"I love you, Papa."

"And I love you."

With a knot in his chest, Andrius bowed his head. The smell of the sea vanished. The sound of the waves receded. And Laurita was gone. The pillow still held the shape of her head; the sheets, her body, but atop the blanket was a single piece of amber in the shape of a tear.

His last, and best, illusion.

He scooped it up and held it to his chest, rocking back and forth. Tears spilled down his cheeks. He held the tiny piece of magic tight and did not let go, not even when the barrel of a gun pressed against his temple.

Glass Boxes and Clockwork Gods

❧ ❧

When the one in red gives up and screams, no one makes a sound. We turn our faces away or rest our foreheads against the glass and wait. It won't take long. Big is quick with the remaking. In between the screams, sharp snaps punctuate the air with exclamation points of splintered bone and leaking marrow.

We all try not to scream.

We all fail in the end.

The walls of our room gleam pale blue speckled with dark spots of dried gore. Little Big is messy. We hang, encased in wood frames with glass fronts and hinged backs, from metal posts embedded in the plaster. Pretty boxes arranged in rows like dolls on a display shelf.

I remember dolls and a small hand in mine.

Big finishes his task and puts the red one back in her box. Swollen lumps of purpled flesh live where her knees used to be, but there is no blood. Big is careful. He hangs her back on the wall and stops, all moonfaced and sweating, in front of my box. The gears on his forehead turn and turn. My heart speeds up four beats in the space of one. His fat mouth opens, revealing crooked tombstone teeth. "Almost perfect," he says, tapping the glass twice before he walks away. My heart stays fast and busy; I know it won't be long before he takes me back out again.

I've been here long enough to forget most of the things I tried so hard to keep. Names. Places. The remaking has taken most of my memories just as sure as it shaped my form into something else. My arms bend in four places now, my legs fold with knees back, my waist is spindle-thin, and my head is too heavy to hold upright. I can't see the changes on the inside, but I hear little clicks and ticks.

Big gathers his tools, wipes down the stained wooden table, and turns out the light before he steps through the doorway, leaving us in shadows and grey. His footsteps thud heavy on the floor, then they fade away to nothing. I don't know what lies beyond the door, beyond this blue room. I think I did know, when my legs bent in the old way, but now I've forgotten.

I crawl into the corner of my box. The sound of muffled weeping from the metal cages hanging on the opposite wall fills the darkness. Those inside the cages used to yell and curse and bang on the bars of their cages, but Little Big took away their mouths, and now they sit, silent mounds of broken flesh, always weeping behind their flat not-mouths. Because they belong to Little Big, they will never have the chance to be perfect.

I want to be perfect. When I am perfect, I will be allowed to leave.

Big remakes the red one's arms next. He puts her back but doesn't take me out. Instead, he fashions three new boxes, tapping the glass into place with a rubber mallet. Then he hangs them, still empty, on the wall and leaves.

I wonder if they will come from the places I've forgotten or someplace else. Someplace I never knew.

Even though there are three empty boxes, Big only brings in two new ones, both dressed in black. One is female, like me; the other, male. They sit in their boxes and whisper words over and over again. The man has a white collar on his neck. I remember we wore collars once, but they had chains attached to them. I don't remember where the chains went.

On the second night, they try to talk to the rest of us. They say, "The old god is dead, killed by the new gods." We cover our ears with our hands to hide the sound, but they are relentless.

Big takes out their tongues first.

After he remakes the red one's legs, Big takes me out of my box and puts me on the table. He runs his fingers along the crosshatch of scars on my pale skin. My hands shake, but he pulls out a shiny box instead of the sharp tools and opens the lid. I remember this box.

"Yes, my pretty one," he says, his voice stretching out to every corner of the room. "You are strong enough now for these."

One by one, he places eight silver rings around my neck, stands me up, and takes away his hands. All the weight inside my skull has turned to air. His ugly teeth open up; laughter spills out.

He hangs me back on the wall. I stand, moving my head from side to side, and inside my neck, the cogs and gears whir a soft, metallic song.

The third box is still empty.

Little Big comes in, and I close my eyes. I don't like his long, narrow face and the skin on his chest pinned back to reveal the metalwork within. A cage door screeches open. I made the mistake of watching his remaking once. The sounds are bad enough—slippery, wet, and scraping. Whenever he finishes, new spots cover the blue wall.

Little Big isn't allowed to touch me, and for this, I am grateful.

The last perfect one was here a long time ago. He wore black rings on his neck, not silver. Big removed the skin on his torso (He didn't scream. He clamped a hand over his mouth and moaned against his palm. I hope I am strong enough to do the same.) and covered the shiny gears with a clear panel.

After he healed, Big carried him out of the blue room forever.

The third box is no longer empty. I smell the new one, all salt-sweat-angry. In the dark, he whispers, "Hello?"

No one answers.

Big lets Little Big watch when he removes the skin from my back. I try to hold in the scream, but I can't. Little Big's eyes light up, and he claps his hands.

"Do you see what I've done?" Big says.

"Many improvements, many indeed," Little Big says, in a thick, raspy voice. "The old design was piss-poor at best."

The new one watches from his box; his eyes are blue, like the wall. Big holds up the panel for my back, shaped thin at the waist with a tiny hole in the center. I think my insides will leak out, but after Big puts in the panel, he attaches a tiny silver key.

It frightens me more than hurt and blood, and I don't know why.

The new one holds in his screams for a long time.

I am healed, but Big hasn't taken me out of the room. He re-makes the red one's waist as tiny as mine and gives the collared man to Little Big. That night, when everyone is quiet, I reach back and touch the key. The perfect man didn't have a key, and I don't understand why I do.

I turn the key to the left, but it won't move, so I turn it to the right. It clicks once, and I bite my lip before a shout can escape. I keep still for a long time, hoping no one else heard the sound.

I turn the key again. One tiny turn. One little click.

The blue-eyed man speaks. "My name is William. What is yours?"

I close my eyes.

"Please. What is your name?"

I have no name. I wait until the darkness swallows up his voice before I sleep.

The one in red dies.

When Big finds her, his shouts and screams fill up the room, loud enough to send echoes through my head. He places her on the table and takes me out of my box. First he wraps a string around my waist, then he holds it around hers, nodding because we are exactly the same.

He leaves me on the table next to her while he opens up her skin. Her icicle fingers brush against mine. On the inside, she is purple and grey and slippery and bits of broken metal. He lifts up each piece. Little Big comes in and laughs; the scratchy sound hurts more than Big's screams. Big pushes him out of the room.

Sharp metal presses against my side, my heart beats crazy-scary-heavy, and the pinch-sting comes. I cry out. Big smiles because I am pink and red and unbroken. He closes me back up with a new line of stitches, black against the white of my skin.

After my skin eats the stitches away, I turn my key again. A sound drifts into the air, a quick little chirp. I hold my breath and look through the gloom. No one moves, no one speaks. The sound lives in my head, not in the room. I turn the key, and a shape takes form in my thoughts, a small shadow moving across a blue not-wall. I know this shape, I remember it. Footsteps thump outside the door, and I close my eyes, my head heavy with chirps and moving shapes and tucked far behind, a sound I don't want to remember.

Little Big leaves but forgets to turn out the lights. The collared man folds his hands together, and his tongueless mouth moves without sound. The blue-eyed man is awake, too, with his remade arms folded across his chest. The new pieces inside him click and spin.

"His prayers won't do any good. Not anymore," he says.

I don't know what a prayer is.

"They're gone for the night," he says. "It's safe to talk."

I shake my head.

"Can you talk?" he asks.

I turn my face away.

"Please," he says. "Talk to me. Tell me your name."

"No," I whisper, cringing at the sound of my own voice, all hard at the edges and soft in the middle.

I turn my key and think of shapes and blue not-walls and a wide expanse of green.

Big remakes the legs of the woman in black but doesn't smile when he finishes. He stops in front of my box and taps on the glass until I look up. He taps the glass again, harder, and then a third time, harder still, and I hear a small sound, like a finger bone cracked in two. The gears on his forehead click to a stop, tick backward, once, twice, and move forward again. With a shake of his head, he walks away.

Little Big breaks the collared man in two pieces and fills in the empty spaces with metal and tangled wire.

I turn my key, and a word rushes in: *Naomi*. Is this the dark shape? I say the word aloud, feel it slip and slide on my tongue.

"Is that your name?" the blue-eyed man asks.

Naomi.

Is it?

Big doesn't come back.

No one will be perfect. No one will leave.

Big tapped the glass too hard, and now there is a crack, a line with shattered edges, all the way at the top. I stay crouched down, away from the crack, turn my key, and remember. The dark shapes were birds that fluttered and circled and sang. A little hand tugged mine, and we ran across the green and under the birds, under the blue not-wall. A pain tugs deep inside where metal and flesh stick together, and I try to turn the key back, to take it away.

I am afraid of what I've forgotten.

I try to pull out the key, but it won't move. I try to bend it, break it, but it is harder than bone.

I am afraid I will never remember.

"Where were you before this place?" His blue eyes are bright under the lights.

"I have always been here."

"Even when you were a child?"

I turn my key. Wide, dark eyes. Chubby fingers. A soft voice whispering.

"I had a daughter with hair the same color as yours. Her name was Lucy. They took her away," he says, his voice breaking in little pieces.

They took me away and made me almost perfect. Maybe they made Lucy perfect and let her go.

"When did you forget?" he asks.

The pain reaches out and my eyes burn.

"Naomi, when did you forget you were human?"

The pain digs in knife-sharp, and I slap the glass with my hands. Big changed most of me, but he left my hands the same. I strike the glass again; a small star blooms at the edge of the crack.

I forgot everything the day I couldn't remember her name. The one with the little hand. I turn the key, but it won't give me her name.

❧   ❧

Little Big smashes the collared one with a hammer. Shards of metal fly up and bounce off my glass, specks of red spatter the walls. He laughs and shakes the hammer in front of our boxes but doesn't break the glass.

"Naomi, you're still human."

Inside, the gears move.

Am I?

"They call themselves gods, you know. Maybe they are, I don't know. They say they killed the old god."

The collared man said the same thing, but the words mean nothing. The key has not shown me god yet.

"They're remaking, changing, everything. The oceans are black now." He laughs, but the edges are hard. "I didn't even believe in god."

I turn my key until I find the ocean, the kiss of water drops on my skin, the salt taste on my lips. She ran into the blue-green water, splashing, and I said, "Be careful, be careful."

"Naomi, please, why won't you talk to me?"

Because I can't remember her name.

Little Big takes the woman in black out of her box and cuts off her arms. He puts her in the cage where the collared one used to live, and she sits in the corner, motionless. She doesn't weep like the others.

In a rush, Little Big leaves the room; I never see him again.

I hit the glass until another star appears.

"Naomi?"

I think about gods and birds and the key in my back. I think about the crack in the glass, how it stretches almost to the bottom now. Every day, *slap-crack*. I think about scars and stitches holding me in place.

Tearing me apart.

I'd like to leave the blue room and see the ocean. I'd like to remember the little one's name. I turn my key, and the gears click.

I'd like to be human again.

❧   ❦

Slap.

Crack.

Until the glass falls like rain. I remember the taste and the way it turned my hair into wet tangles. Before they took me away, before the remaking and the pain. There are still holes in my memory, spaces for forgotten things, but I remember enough, and if Big finds me, I won't let him put me back in the box.

I step to the edge. Thick dust covers the wooden table and the floor and shimmers like a grey veil. I think we are the forgotten things now. Broken, remade into almost perfect, yet left behind.

"Naomi, be careful," the one with the blue eyes says.

William. His name is William.

"I will," I say.

I will break his glass, too, and find a way to free the others. I won't leave anyone behind. I hope my legs are strong enough to break my fall, but I am not afraid.

I remember her name.

Sugar, Sin,
and Nonsuch Henry

❧ ❦

Sugarsin bumped into Henry VIII at a yard sale.

One minute she was making her way between two tables draped with a floral cloth and loaded with a haphazard array of junk; the next, she rounded the table, and her shoulder struck something hard and unyielding. She said, "Sorry," glanced up, and froze in place.

He'd been placed off to the side like an afterthought, next to a wrought iron coat rack and an umbrella stand in the shape of a penguin. No one had bothered to wipe the dust from his face or brush the cobwebs from his hair, and dark stains riddled his doublet and hose. At least his codpiece was intact.

In spite of the grime, there was no mistaking his visage, captured in the prime of his youth before he went to fat and ruin and rage. She checked the nape of his neck, under his hair, and smiled. The factory seal remained intact, which meant no one had altered his programming. He was an older model, an unsuccessful one, despite the massive media campaigns. Too old-fashioned for anyone but the faux-flesh collectors.

And for her.

The company called them historical companions—*to amuse your friends and family*. Sugarsin always thought it would be interesting, albeit strange, to have one, but even after the price on the Henry model was reduced by half, it was still more expensive than she could afford. She thought of her house, the quiet; it might be nice to have some signs of life, even of the artificial variety. And how many strippers could claim to have a Tudor king in residence?

She took a step back and bumped into another shoulder, this one attached to a living man with sculpted biceps, a cleft chin, and hair artfully dyed grey at the temples.

"Interested?" the man asked.

"Yes, I am," she said with a smile. "Can I ask why you're selling him? Does he still work?"

"He worked fine the last time we turned him on. He was a gift for my wife, but she hated him. They wouldn't take him back, so he's been in the attic ever since. We don't have the manual anymore, though, but I think you can probably find it online." His eyes, an unnaturally bright shade of green, dropped down to her cleavage, then back up with a grin.

"How much are you asking?"

"If you can carry him yourself, you can have him for free."

Sugarsin bit her lower lip. Free usually meant broken, but what the hell. She could clean up his clothes and put him in the corner of her living room. "Okay, I'll take him."

The man nodded. "Good, good. My wife will be happy. His accent was too heavy for her to understand so I got her a John Wayne instead."

Sugarsin laughed out loud.

Despite his earlier statement, he ended up helping her carry Henry to her car.

Once home, she paid the neighbor's son to help bring him in. She found the on switch located in the center of his back but hesitated. After being offline for so long, he'd need to stay on for at least twelve hours, and she had to get ready for work. She pushed a strand of ginger hair out of his eyes. They didn't use real human hair on all the models (it was an extra, and pricey, option), but she was lucky.

She removed his clothing to run it through the wash. Nude and anatomically correct, he gave the appearance of a sleepwalking man who had wandered into her house and paused while his dreams caught up. A cold shiver traced its way down her spine. No, he wasn't a man; he was a robot and nothing more.

"All right, Henry," she whispered. "We'll get you setup tomorrow."

When Sugarsin walked through the door at Whirlygigs, the gaze of the new bouncer followed her until the dressing room door shut. She was something of an oddity, the only natural at the club; all the other women wore enhancements like a second skin. In Lulu's case, her enhancement *was* skin, a removable artificial layer of ivory pale to cover up freckles and other unacceptable imperfections. Silicone and injectables still remained high on the list of wanted, and expected, adjustments, but technology moved faster than tips on a Saturday night.

Born two years before fetal manipulation was approved, Sugarsin had genetic luck on her side, and thanks to her mother's alcohol-induced sense of humor, she didn't need a stage name.

Mouth set in a tight line, she pulled a costume from her bag. She was dressing as Anne Boleyn tonight, more than fitting. Although *she'd* get to keep her head.

She had the right hair for the part, no wig required, but her eyes were the wrong color, not that it mattered. The men and women who came to the club didn't care about the costumes—she could go on stage with a burlap sack—they wanted what was underneath.

Once dressed, she adjusted the choker around her neck and waited by the stage curtain with the vibration of the heavy techno music thumping through her body. In her gown, she felt like a displaced time traveler. New dancers always looked askance at her costumes, but the owner indulged her choices because she had a steady, loyal, and well-paying clientele, attracted to the real.

The music stopped, and after a few minutes of applause, Miria stepped through the curtain, wiping sweat from her forehead. Her enhancements included a set of tits the size of baby torpedoes. What the clients couldn't see was the internal system used to hold them upright, a fine net-like material that ran from the implants, over her shoulders and down to her waist, anchored with screws into her spine.

"Your boys are here, Sugar," Miria said with a grin. "I warmed them up for you."

Sugarsin's music started, and she stretched up high on her toes, rotated her shoulders back and around, and shook out her hands. This was the easy part. After her show, she had to go out, chat up the customers, and pretend she didn't mind their hands trying to creep under her robe to cop a feel.

She put on a smile and moved through the curtain, slow and

lazy in her long gown, the very picture of Tudor loveliness. Except for the lace g-string underneath, of course.

Sugarsin redressed Henry, checked his factory imprint again, and wrote down his model and serial number. While she drank coffee and searched for the manual online, her feet tapped out an impatient rhythm, stilling once the manual opened up on her screen. She read for half an hour, her coffee turning cold and forgotten.

"Okay, Henry," she whispered. "Let's see if you work."

She pushed the on/off button hard and held it for the required thirty seconds, designed that way so it couldn't be pushed accidentally. If someone had Elvis serving drinks to their dinner guests, it wouldn't do to have an errant pat on the back result in total shutdown and spilled martinis.

Inside Henry, a tiny click sounded, then a subtle whir. The synthetic skin warmed beneath her hand. After another click, another whir, his hands closed into fists, then relaxed. His eyes opened. He blinked.

"I like her not," he said, his blue eyes narrowing. His voice held a deep, rich resonance, his accent heavy, though not difficult to understand.

Sugarsin stepped back.

"Blighted in the eyes of God."

"Well, hello to you, too," she mumbled, crossing her arms across her chest.

"If it were not to satisfy the world, and my Realm, I would not do that I must do this day for none earthly thing."

"No wonder people didn't like you. Keep it up and I'll shut you off, stick you in the corner, and dress you up with string lights."

He gave a small bow. "Good morrow. I am Henry VIII, by the Grace of God, King of England, France, and Ireland, Defender of the Faith and of the Church of England."

"Yes, I know."

He cocked his head to the side. "Of course. How could you not?"

"I have a feeling you're going to be a handful."

He lifted his chin, but said nothing. Instead, he walked around the room with his hands clasped behind his back. When he stopped at her bookcases, she looked down and nudged the carpet with her toe. More than half the books were accounts of the Tudor dynasty, with more than half of those focused solely on Henry VIII.

"Are you fond of history?" he asked over his shoulder.

"Sometimes."

"*Tudor* history?"

"Sometimes."

She followed him into the kitchen, where his only comment was a wry "No servants?" into the dining room, and up the stairs. He paused in front of the picture in the hallway, a reproduction of Hans Holbein's *Henry VIII after 1537*, peered into the small spare bedroom, the bathroom, and then her bedroom, where her costume from the previous night hung from a hook on the wall.

He stepped into the room. "Do you also sometimes have a fondness for dressing as historical figures?"

"It's a costume for work," Sugarsin said.

"And what do you do?"

"I'm a dancer."

He turned. "A dancer. What sort of dance do you perform?" he asked with a smile.

In that moment, Sugarsin could see why the real Henry had charmed a legion of women, even if the construct had only a tenth of the charisma of the real man. "The sort with no clothes."

One eyebrow raised. "That must be…challenging."

Sugarsin laughed.

"My dear lady, I fear I've been remiss. May I ask your name?"

"Sugarsin."

The eyebrow raised again. "Sugarsin. I quite like it."

He paced back and forth while he recited a long poem about the divine right of kings, his voice rising and falling with each line. She read passages from several books on Tudor history, and he scoffed at the differing opinions in each book, until she read from a fairly obscure tome that contradicted nearly everything in the earlier narratives. He took the book from her hand and tossed it aside. "I like it not," he said.

She settled him into the spare bedroom. According to the manual, he needed several hours of system downtime, a state that resembled sleep (minus the snoring, tossing, and turning) to recharge. When she bid him goodnight, he trailed his fingers through the ends of her hair and lifted his hand to her cheek, but she pulled away before his fingers made contact.

"I'd like to see you dance with no clothes."

"I'd like you to keep writing whatever it is you're writing and let me finish my coffee."

He pushed the chair back from the kitchen table and held his hand out over the paper. "It is another poem."

"More divine rights?"

"No, a discussion of children and their fathers. Tell me of your father."

Sugarsin set down her coffee mug. "I never knew him."

"Are you a bastard, then?"

She ran her finger along the edge of the table. "Good question. I don't know. If they were married, my mother never mentioned it. He split when I was two, and I never saw him again."

"Have you any memories of him?"

"No."

"'Tis a pity. Are you close with your mother?"

Sugarsin shook her head. Hard. "No. Tell me more about what you're writing."

"When are you going to allow me into your bed?"

She choked down a mouthful of coffee. "What?"

"You've given me no tasks to perform, no parties to attend to. You have neither a husband nor a lover, so I assume I am here to warm your bed."

"You assume wrong."

"Oh? Do your tastes align with commoners, then? Most women would give almost anything to bed a king."

"I'm not most women. And anyway, several women gave up their *lives* when they bedded Henry VIII, in case you've forgotten."

"But I am a false king, am I not? Do you prefer to bed women?"

"No, I don't prefer women."

"No husband, no women. Are you frigid?"

Sugarsin slapped her hand down on the table. "Enough."

"As you wish," he said. "Milady. Will you tell me why you're so enraptured with Tudor history?"

She shrugged. "The tragedy, I suppose. They had everything, money and power, and it wasn't enough. It should've been, but it wasn't."

He didn't say a word, only nodded in response.

Later, he watched her put makeup on and pack costumes in her bag.

"Why are you taking those, if you dance with no clothes?"

"Because I wear them first, then they come off."

He touched the sleeve of her Anne Boleyn dress. "Are you not taking this one?"

"No, not tonight."

"Do you believe she loved him?"

Sugarsin tossed her hairbrush in the bag. "Do you think *he* loved *her*?"

"I should think so, at least to some extent."

"Not enough," she said.

"Enough, though, to make her a queen."

"But not enough to keep him from having her head cut off when he grew tired of her—what a nice guy—but you already know this. It's in your programming."

He smiled and folded his arms across his chest. "On light pretexts, by false accusations, they made me put to death the most faithful servant I ever had."

Sugarsin smiled. "Good King Hal said that after he had Cromwell's head chopped off."

"A terrible mistake, that, and one he regretted for the rest of his days."

"Well, he made quite a few mistakes during his reign," she said.

"Why do you think it so?"

She tapped one finger against her chin. "Because he had absolute power. If someone said or did something he didn't like, he had their heads cut off or their guts torn open."

Henry nodded. "No one should have that sort of power. Over anyone." He crossed his arms and rocked back on his heels. "Are there many like me?"

"What do you mean?"

"Are there many Henrys like me?"

She shook her head. "No, you weren't a popular model."

"And why is that, pray tell?"

Sugarsin zipped up her bag and turned to face Henry. The overhead light gave his eyes a mirror-like shine. "Because you're sort of an ass."

"Hmmph. Why did they make me that way?"

"They try to be as realistic as possible with the programming. I mean, if someone wants Elvis, they want him, not just a looka-like. They can go to Vegas for that."

"Is Elvis popular?"

"Very."

"I take it as a personal affront that a singer is more popular than a king. Especially one such as I."

"And there you go. Arrogance isn't attractive, even for a false king."

"How presumptuous, then, are you, to find fault with your Prince."

Sugarsin groaned, picked up her bag, and pushed past him.

When she got home, Henry was already in the spare bedroom with the door shut. Sugarsin lay awake for a long time watching shadows playdance on the ceiling. The weight of another person's presence, even an artificial one, hung heavy in the air.

She bought him new clothes and took him to the park. Perfect, beautiful children were running in circles, their mothers, all enhanced in some fashion, busy calling out names and setting up picnic lunches.

They sat below a willow tree, half-hidden by the branches. He watched the children play, laughing at their antics. After a time, he turned. Smiled. "Do you wish to have children?"

"No."

"And why not?"

Below the children's round, cherubic cheeks, high cheekbones waited. Below their slim torsos, perfect curves for the girls and wide shoulders for the boys. And if anything didn't turn out quite right, doctors were ready and willing to add or subtract where needed.

She thought of her mother. The secret bottles stashed under the sofa; the liquor-slap of hands before Sugarsin learned how to avoid them; the drunken slurs and at times, the strange men who wandered in and out of her mother's life, ignoring her young daughter, if said daughter was lucky.

"I'm not the motherly type."

"Why have you neither husband nor lover?" he asked, his voice low.

"Because I choose not to."

"Most people wish to have a companion, no?"

"I suppose so, but I prefer to be alone."

"But now you have me."

"Yes, but you're not real."

He said nothing in return.

She woke in the middle of the night, twisted in her sheets. Henry stood by her bed.

"I do not wish to be an ass," he said.

Sugarsin wiped sleep from her eyes. "What?"

"I would like not to be a king, even a false one."

"I don't understand."

"No matter. I am sorry to have disturbed your sleep," he said, and closed her door.

By morning, she'd convinced herself it had been a dream; she found a fresh pot of coffee in the kitchen and a note next to her coffee mug.

I've gone for a walk.

H.

He returned several hours later and without a word, went upstairs to his bedroom and shut the door with a quiet click. She curled up on the sofa with a book, but closed it after a few pages and turned on a movie instead.

She didn't see him at all the following day, although she heard him moving about in his room, and before she left for work, she knocked on his door. "Is everything okay?"

"Quite so," he said.

She returned home several hours later to find Henry waiting in the living room. He handed her a glass of wine and sat next to her, silent, while she drank. Once the glass was empty, he led her upstairs and pressed a chaste kiss to her cheek. "Good night," he whispered before disappearing into his room.

She gave a small laugh and climbed into bed.

Another note sat on the kitchen counter.

I've gone out.

H.

He returned with a bouquet of flowers, and presented them to her with a low bow.

"Thank you," she said.

"You are most welcome."

He cooked her dinner, using recipes he found online.

"What's the occasion?" she asked, after he led her to the table.

"No occasion at all," he said and poured her a glass of wine. "I wanted to cook for you, so I did."

After she ate, he took her hand. "Walk with me."

"Where?"

"Outside. In the fresh air."

They ended up in the park, walking in aimless circles where they'd watched the children play. On their way home, she stumbled on a bit of cracked pavement; he caught her before she fell to the ground and kept his arm around her the rest of the way home.

When they shut the front door behind them, he leaned over and pressed his lips to hers. He tasted of lemons. They walked upstairs together, but he pushed her gently into her room and shut the door between them.

He liked to brush her hair and when the strands were tangle free, run his fingers through it over and over again. He whispered to her in French, laughing at her frustration when he wouldn't translate, wrote poem after poem, and read Shakespeare aloud, an anachronism she found amusing. He made her desserts topped with whipped cream. He massaged her back and shoulders when she got home from work.

One night, after a game of Scrabble, she took his hand and led him upstairs into her room. Later, in the dark, she rested her head on his chest listening to the absence of a heartbeat.

"Are you going to be an ass now that you've gotten me into your bed?" she whispered.

He kissed the top of her head. "Milady, we are in *your* bed."

She slept a dreamless sleep, and in the morning, he brought her a cup of coffee exactly the way she liked it.

Sugarsin smiled on the outside and trembled on the in.

"There's someone here to see you," Lulu called from the doorway.

Sugarsin looked up from the mirror, a tube of eyeliner in her hand. "A customer?"

"I don't think so. At least I've never seen him here before. He's tall with reddish hair?"

Sugarsin's hands curled into fists. Maybe Lulu was mistaken. The dressing room door slid shut behind her without a sound. She stepped into the hallway and paused before the curtain, peeking out between the panels.

"Shit," she muttered.

She tightened the sash around her robe and stepped out into the club, dodging offers of drinks as she moved to Henry's table.

"What are you doing here?" she asked.

"I wanted to see where you worked."

"How did you get here?"

"I walked, of course."

"Okay, well this is where I work. You can go home now."

"I would like to see you dance."

"No. Not here like this."

"Why not?"

"Because this is my job, okay?"

"I do not understand."

She lowered her voice. "I don't want people to see you here."

A bouncer came over to the table. "Is there a problem here?" He folded his arms over his chest, his brass-plated knuckles gleaming under the lights.

"No, there's no problem. He was just leaving."

Henry lifted his chin, but stood up. He gave her a curt bow. "Good evening, both of you."

"New boyfriend?" The bouncer asked when he walked away.

"No. He's no one. No one at all."

She didn't speak a word to Henry when she got home, simply walked in and went upstairs to her bedroom. When the door clicked shut, a cold chill traced its way up her spine. She heard his footsteps on the stairs and felt his presence just beyond the door.

"What have I done to anger you so?"

"Nothing."

Everything.

She flipped the lock and waited until he walked away.

"I wish you would speak to me. I love you."

She bit back a laugh.

"What is so amusing?"

"You're a robot, okay? You aren't real. You can't fall in love. Did you really think we were going to walk off into the sunset together?"

His eyes narrowed. "Why are you so afraid to feel?"

She stalked out of the room, her hands shaking.

He came up behind her later while she stood at the kitchen window, staring out at the shadows in the yard. His arms wrapped around her, and he pressed a kiss to the top of her head.

"I am sorry I upset you."

Tears blurred her vision. She never should have taken him out of the house or let him into her bed or make her breakfast. It had to be a default in his programming. He couldn't possibly feel. It was a cruel joke.

"If I were real, would you let me in?" he whispered.

But she didn't want anyone to let anyone in, real or not. That led only to tears and heartache and loneliness.

She turned and rested her head on his shoulder. The tears spilled down her cheeks. Her hands curved around his back, and she ran her fingers over the spot concealing the on/off switch. One push would turn him back into a statue. Into nothing.

No one should have that sort of power over anyone.

One little push.

Part II

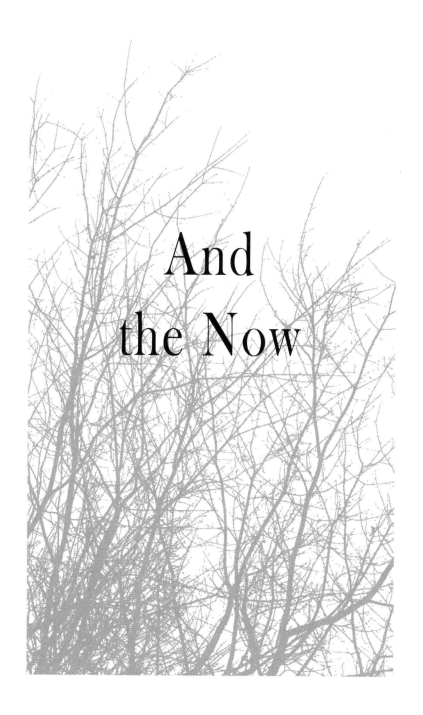

And
the Now

Running Empty in a Land of Decay

❧ ❦

The first few miles of any run are the hardest. Your muscles protest and your lungs scream, but once you push past all the hurt, you get to the good part, the part where the world zips by in bright flashes of color and your conscious thoughts fade away. In that zone, you hear, but don't hear; see, but don't see. You breathe in and out, moving forward. Moving on. You might even try to catch that elusive four-minute mile. You don't look back or pause to gaze at the scenery. You just head for that finish line, whether it's an actual line, a mile marker, or the end of a street.

When I run now, with the pedometer clicking away the steps and the miles, I pretend everything is normal. I pretend I'm not running away, even though there's nothing left to run away from.

But I can't turn off my thoughts anymore.

It's been a long time since I've seen one of the dead. Months, maybe a year, maybe longer than that. Hard to tell; time is funny now. They're nothing more than a few scraps of putrescent flesh lingering here and there. They came with limited mileage, like running shoes.

It's been even longer since I've seen anyone alive.

The streets here are clear. No cars. No rotting bodies. No potholes. My feet keep moving, the rhythm steady and sure.

Mike always said running was my obsession. That obsession saved my life more than once. More than the gun I still carry in my backpack, even though I don't need it anymore. Curse me for a fool, even when all I saw were bodies, bloodstains on pavement, and torn clothing blowing in the wind like farewell handkerchiefs, I kept running, hoping I'd find someone else.

And then I didn't have a reason to stop.

Mike and I survived the first few months barricaded in our apartment. A lot of folks left San Francisco in the beginning; most of the dead followed suit, following the food source. We took turns making supply runs, up until the day he came back with a bite on his arm. I pretended he was immune and wouldn't die, but he wasn't and he did.

When Mike reopened his eyes, he wasn't there. The stranger wearing his face staggered toward me, all gnashing teeth and furious hunger.

I shot him in the head. I could barely see through my tears, but I didn't hesitate. He'd made me promise not to.

Before he fell to the floor, I saw a flash of the real Mike deep inside; for one quick second, his open mouth wasn't a gaping maw of destruction, but a smile.

At least I'd like to think so.

It doesn't matter now. Nothing does, nothing except my shoes hitting the pavement, one after the other, and the breeze, thick with the salt tang of the ocean.

I left my original pair of shoes, flecked with blood and gore, next to Mike's body. I picked up this pair a couple of hundred miles back. Funny how no one touched the running stores; I guess they didn't realize the importance of good shoes.

I've left shoes along the way, every three hundred miles or so, always with the scuffed toes pointing east. I left one pair on the edge of an empty water fountain in Utah, another next to a cornfield in Kansas, and still another by a railroad track in Missouri. I left the pair that gave me a blister in Kentucky, right before I crossed into Virginia.

I forget where I left the others. It's hard to keep track. Everything is the same: empty streets, vacant houses with broken windows, the awful silence.

And the sick-sweet stink of rot.

Except here. The breeze floats by again. Salt and sea. No decay. I pick up my pace. It's not a four-minute mile or even a fiver, but it's brisk enough.

I should've left notes in the shoes, so anyone who found them would at least know my name. Except there's no one left. I know that, even when I pretend I don't.

The roar of the waves crashes in on the quiet, a lullaby beckoning me forward. I've never seen the Atlantic Ocean in person. I know it's colder than the Pacific and grey-green instead of blue, but there are no memories here. No Mike, no gunshot echoing off the plaster walls, no running from the dead with their bloody mouths and reaching hands, and no useless hope.

I sit down on the curb, my muscles quivering, and unlace my shoes. My last pair. I leave my socks and the pedometer on the pavement and tie my shoelaces together in a double knot. I set them next to the socks, but after a few seconds, pick them back up. What's the point?

A knot tightens in my chest; tears blur my vision. I scramble to my feet. With a shout, I throw the shoes up, over my shoulder. A series of dull taps fills the air.

I spin around.

Caught by the laces, the shoes are hanging from a dead power line, swaying back and forth.

I was here, they say.

And no one will ever know.

I turn away, the tears flowing down my cheeks. Eventually the laces will rot and the shoes will fall. I hope they land pointing in the right direction.

The sand, warm and cool at the same time, slips between my toes as I make my way across the beach, walking now, not running. The water shimmers in the sunlight. Maybe it will wash everything away. All the miles. All the blood. All the hurt.

After that, maybe I'll move into one of the beach houses, gather supplies and books, and relax for a decade or three. Or maybe I'll stay in the water and head out until the waves spill over my head. Until the undertow tugs me away.

I don't know.

But I'm not running anymore.

Scarred

❧ ❧

Violet carved her hate into her flesh one name at a time. Her skin was riddled with scars, some barely visible, others dark and ruddy. The oldest, the first name, was on her right ankle, above the knobby bone. It revealed a halting progress, with many gaps in between the lines and curves.

He suffered for a long time.

Anthony looked up from his dinner plate and smiled. "This is really good, babe."

"Thank you. I wanted to make something special for tonight."

The cooking classes were her idea. Anthony had been worried about the knives, of course, although he hadn't said anything with his mouth. Only with his eyes. The first time his hand had touched one of her scars, he'd paused, his eyes curious. Concerned.

She'd looked down at her hands. "I had a…problem when I was younger, but I'm better now."

"What do they mean?"

"Nothing," she'd said. "Nothing at all."

A breeze blew in through the open windows, fluttering the curtains, and the late spring air was heavy with the scent of flowers. Children's voices called out, and their neighbor's dog barked several times, a deep, growling sort of bark. She and Anthony grimaced at the same time, caught each other, and smiled.

"Happy anniversary, babe," he said.

"Happy anniversary."

She smiled and twisted the ring on her finger. The year had passed so quickly, yet seemed a lifetime. Anthony had asked her to marry him on their sixth date. Crazy, perhaps, because they'd barely known each other, but she'd said yes without a second thought. Three weeks later, they were standing hand in hand in the courthouse promising forever, a promise she intended to keep.

Mrs. Anthony Cardno was a good person.

But Violet isn't, and you know it.

That wasn't true. She *was* a good person. Sometimes she got…lost. That was all. But it was all in the past. She was better now. So much better.

With Anthony softly snoring in the bed beside her, Violet clasped her hands together on her chest and recited the names. Too many names.

"Please forgive me," she whispered when she was finished.

She rolled onto her side and touched Anthony's cheek, his skin soft, yet rough at the same time, beneath her fingertips. The sleeve of her pajama top slipped up to her elbow, revealing the edge of a name: *Sabrina.* Her best friend in grade school. Violet closed her eyes.

It wasn't her fault. She hadn't meant to hurt anyone. She hadn't known.

Liar.

She woke before Anthony and padded down to the kitchen to make coffee. From the kitchen window, she saw the next door neighbor's children, already up and about, kicking around a red rubber ball. She smiled and touched her belly. Two months ago, she'd thrown out her birth control pills and while nothing had happened yet, they were both young. There was plenty of time. Anthony would be a wonderful father, and she would be a good mother even if the baby didn't sleep well or cried all the time.

"You were always crying when you were a baby," her mother had said time and again. "Drove me crazy. You'd cry if you were hungry or full, wet or dry, it didn't matter. It was like you came out hating the world and wanted everyone to know it." Her mother would tap her cigarette into her overflowing ashtray, pat Violet on the bum, and smile. "Grab me another beer, okay?"

When her mother had married her stepfather, Violet had hoped that everything would be okay. Now she had a real family. Her mother would be happy, wouldn't drink so much, and wouldn't forget to go food shopping or pay the electric bill. But her stepfather had only made things worse. So much worse.

But we took care of him, didn't we?

No, no matter what he'd done, he didn't deserve what happened. No one did.

Long after the sun had faded from the sky, she and Anthony took a walk through the neighborhood. The children and dogs had been collected for the night, and lights behind windows winked out one by one. His hand gave hers a quick squeeze.

"Next year we'll go away someplace for our anniversary. How does that sound? Somewhere with a beach and blue water."

"And fruity drinks with paper umbrellas?"

"Absolutely."

He pulled her into his arms and kissed her softly beneath the glow of a streetlamp. Then they heard the shout. She jumped, pulled away, and scanned the street. No one else was outside. The shout came again, more muffled this time, from a small green house with a swing on the front porch.

Anthony took a step toward the house. Violet shook her head.

"Don't."

"But if someone is hurt…"

A voice snapped in anger, followed by a whip-quick sound that Violet knew all too well—a slap.

"Let's go back home."

Anthony gave the house a long look. Violet tugged his hand.

"Come on. It's not our business."

Violet was collecting her mail from the mailbox at the end of the yard when a dark-haired woman and a little girl of perhaps four or five in a yellow dress and white ruffled socks walked past. She looked up just in time to see the bruise darkening the skin of the woman's cheek. Violet's hands clenched into fists. The little girl pulled her thumb out of her mouth and offered up a wide, innocent smile.

You can make things better.

No, it wasn't her fight. She didn't know them at all. She watched them turn onto the sidewalk leading up to the green house.

But you could if you really wanted to. Just one more time. Help them, then I'll go away.

The voice whispered so sweetly, but it lied. Oh, how it lied.

Violet pulled out a knife to slice tomatoes for a salad and paused. The overhead light glinted in the metal. She closed her eyes and saw the little girl's face, the woman's bruise.

You can fix it.

"Leave me alone," she whispered.

Two years after her mother had married her stepfather, the voice spoke to her for the first time. Eight-year-old Violet had been sitting in the corner of her bedroom with the door locked, wiping tears away, with a fresh set of bruises on her upper arms.

"I hate you," she whispered. Over and over again.

I can help you, a voice said.

She'd jumped up, stifling a shout, looked under the bed, checked inside the closet and out the window. The voice had laughed softly.

I won't hurt you.

She'd covered her ears. Buried her face in the pillow.

Trust me. It will be easy. So easy.

It had whispered and whispered, and eventually her hands had dropped from her ears. It had told her what to do, and when the house had fallen silent, Violet had tiptoed to the kitchen and pulled out a small knife.

Good girl. That's a very good girl.

She'd closed her eyes when she had touched the blade to her ankle, and the pain had not been nearly as bad as she'd imagined it would be. Beneath the copper bright tang of blood, she'd smelled something dark and terrible like the sweet stink of roadkill or the scummy water left in a vase filled with dead flowers. She'd felt something light brush against her skin, opened her eyes, and saw a shadow flickering across the floor. One quick flicker, and then it was gone.

She didn't know then what it would do.

A few days later, her stepfather had collapsed in the backyard. The doctors had called it a rare, aggressive cancer, but Violet had known they were wrong. The malignant cells hadn't eaten him away from the inside. Her hate had.

Let me out.

She dropped the knife back into the drawer and slammed it shut. It bounced back open with a little jingle, offering her a hint of the silverware within.

"No!"

She took several long deep breaths. She would not do it. Not now. Not ever. She recited the names. Once. Twice.

"I am sorry. I am so sorry."

Words. Useless words. Her stepfather had said them so many times.

He wasn't really sorry. You weren't, either.

Standing in front of the green house, Violet noticed the white letter sticking out of the mailbox. She stepped closer, casting quick glances over both shoulders. The letter was out far enough for her to make out a name—*Kevin Turner.*

With her mouth set into a thin line, she turned and walked back to her own house, the name a heavy weight inside. She couldn't hate him. She didn't even know him.

You could if you wanted to. He's just like your stepfather.

She didn't know that. The woman could have fallen down. How many times had she done something stupid, something that—

Excuses, excuses. You know you want to. That's why you looked at the letter.

No, it wasn't that way at all. She wouldn't do anything. She'd promised to leave it all behind. For Anthony's sake. For her own sake.

Sabrina Ogden had been her best friend all through grade school. In their first year of middle school, Violet had spoken of what her stepfather had done. Sabrina had told another friend who told another and on and on. The whispers had followed Violet through the hallways. The shame had burned like a brand.

When the dark voice had whispered, Violet had tried to hold it in, but she hadn't been strong enough.

The doctors hadn't been able to cure Sabrina, either.

Tears burned in Violet's eyes.

If she'd been your friend, she wouldn't have told anyone. If she hadn't—

"Violet?"

She jumped, and the paring knife in her hands clattered into the kitchen sink. She stared at the blade for several long moments, her mouth dry. She didn't remember opening the silverware drawer. Did she?

You know you want to. I've been waiting for so long.

She slipped on a smile and turned around.

"You looked like you were a million miles away," Anthony said.

"Sorry, I was woolgathering."

She went to him and rested her head on his chest.

In the dark, she stared up at the ceiling. Recited the names.

Joey, who'd tried to take advantage of her at a party in high school. Sarah, that same year, who'd blackened her eye and fractured her wrist for telling the principal about the smoking in the bathroom. Christopher. Laura. Matt. Jake, who'd broken her heart. Peter, who'd shattered it. Ryan, who'd promised to love her forever. He hadn't deserved to die such a terrible death.

And so many more. She wanted to forget them all, but she held tight, fearing she would.

My fault, my fault. All of them, she thought.

Every time she'd carved a name, the darkness reappeared, a slithering shadow she could only see as a human-shaped haze in the air. Did they see it come for them? Did they taste its fate in their breath?

And did they know she'd sent it?

Just one more time. Please.

"Stop it, stop it, stop it."

She didn't want to hurt anyone. She was a good person now. She *was*.

Violet saw the little girl again, playing in the front yard of the green house. She was digging in the dirt with a stick, singing softly to herself. When she heard Violet's footsteps, she glanced up, and Violet saw bruises on her forearm, four finger-shaped marks. Violet's hands curled into fists. Her heart beat heavy in her chest.

We can help her.

No, it was not her problem. But her steps were heavy on her walk back home.

An image of the girl's bruises floated in Violet's mind, and her fingers tightened on her open book.

One more time. I promise I'll go away.

Why wouldn't it just leave her alone?

You know you want to help her.

But not in that way. She would call Child Protective Services in the morning. They could help the little girl.

What if they don't?

The words on the page swam into a blur. She recited the names. Ran the tip of her finger over the edge of a scar. Recited the names again.

Her cup of guilt was deep, the brew within thick and bitter. No matter how many swallows, she could never drink it all down. Not in one lifetime or ten.

"Honey, are you okay?"

Violet looked up from her book. "Yes, why?"

"You had the strangest expression on your face."

"I was just focused on the story, I guess."

He touched the back of her hand.

"If something is bothering you, you can tell me. You know that, right?"

"Of course I do."

She put her hand atop his. The words gathered in her throat, but she swallowed them down. Anthony was the first, the only, good thing in her life. If he knew the truth, the things she'd done, he'd run as far away as possible.

Violet put the phone down, her mouth set in a thin line.

They won't help her, and you know it.

But they would. The woman on the phone said they would send someone out. A snippet of memory crept in. A woman from CPS came to her house once, and in spite of the bruises on Violet, she hadn't done anything except write a report. But things were different now; they took bruises more seriously. The little girl would be okay.

But you can make sure of it.

Violet sagged against the counter and groaned into her hands.

"Leave me alone, please, just leave me alone."

Never.

But she already knew that. It would never go away. Never give her peace. She was broken. Wrong. She yanked the silverware drawer open and grabbed a knife.

"Is this what you want?"

Yes. You know you want it, too.

No. She wanted to be well, to be happy.

She made a tiny cut.

Yesss...

"No! I will not do this. I will *not.*"

She threw the knife down, sank down with her back against a cabinet, and put her head in her hands. Recited the names. A harsh sob bubbled up from deep inside her chest. The names. The deaths. All her fault. She was a monster. With a grimace, she scrambled for the knife.

You want this. You know you do.

She slashed at her skin, her grimace turning into a smile at the sharp, beautiful sting of the knife. Even that was wrong. It never hurt enough. She cut again and again, the letters distorted. Wet, red mouths dripping crimson pearls. When she finished, she threw the knife down.

"Are you happy now?"

And there, on the delicate skin of her wrist—*Violet.*

One last name, one last death, to pay for them all.

What did you do? You stupid, stupid woman.

Tears blurred her vision as the blood dripped to the floor.

"Please forgive me, Anthony," she whispered, her voice small and insignificant in the quiet. "It's so much better this way. You deserve someone so much better."

No, no, no! You can't do this. You cannot!

She had to. It was the only way. Her limbs filled with lassitude, her mouth dropped open, and her breath came long and slow.

A shadow emerged from the wound like a ribbon, taking shape as it grew. It slipped free slowly, ponderously, its weight feather-light, its stench thick and heavy. It caressed her cheek in a hideous lover's pantomime. She took a deep breath, steeled herself against the pain to come, yet the shadow slithered across the tile, moving away from her without a sound.

"No, no, no."

She reached out, but her fingers passed through the darkness. She grabbed again and again, caught nothing but a kiss of air against her skin. Then the shadow slipped beneath the door, and she sobbed into her hands. She didn't understand. She'd carved her name. Why didn't it take her? She rocked back and forth, her arms wrapped around her knees. No voice whispered in her mind. Only a strange, calm silence. Could it have been that easy all along? But all those deaths...

No. It had to come back for her. It *had* to make her pay.

Ambulance lights cut the night with slashes of red and blue, and Anthony's hand gripped Violet's tight, his skin warm against hers. The neighbors watched from their porches, their eyes filled with curious alarm as the paramedics wheeled a stretcher out of the green house.

"I wonder what happened," Anthony whispered.

Violet rubbed her finger along the cut on her wrist, still in the pink of healing. A few moments later, the dark-haired woman stepped out of the house, her face expressionless, the little girl by her side. And on the girl's ankle, not quite covered by a white ruffled sock, Violet saw the name carved into her flesh: *Daddy*.

No, oh, no. A chill raced down Violet's spine. Her mouth went dry.

Anthony tugged her hand.

"Come on, let's go back home."

Violet heard his voice as if from far away. She couldn't move, couldn't take her eyes away from the little girl.

"Violet, honey, what's wrong?"

The little girl met Violet's gaze, her lips curved into a dark, familiar smile. A smile laced with hate.

The Taste of Tears
in a Raindrop

☙ ❧

Alec woke to the sound of crying.

"Megan?"

He blinked once, twice, and the still unfamiliar room swam from sleep-blurry to clear. Megan wasn't in this house; she was at his old house with his ex-wife, or soon-to-be ex, anyway.

Still, *someone* was crying. Not the tears of an eight-year-old awakened by a nightmare, but the hitching, almost silent sobbing of the brokenhearted or the distressed.

Between the slats of the blinds, he saw the woman in the backyard, the night breeze carrying the sound of her sorrow in through the open window. She stood with her back toward the house, her arms wrapped close around her body, her head bowed.

He frowned, pushing the plastic slats almost to the breaking point. Although he'd only moved into the rental house last week and hadn't met any of the neighbors yet, he'd seen some of them come and go, and none looked like this.

The woman wore a dress in a deep, yet vibrant, shade of blue, the color of an ocean in a far off country. The gauzy fabric hung in loose folds and pooled around her feet; her long dark hair was caught up in some sort of clip that caught the moonlight every time her shoulders hitched. She turned her face up toward the window, and he saw the curve of her cheek, wet with tears, and the dark of her eyes. Her nose was strong and angular, her cheekbones sharply defined, the bone structure reminiscent of old statues, her skin marble pale. She was striking, *present*, in a way that made it hard for him to breathe.

It didn't answer the question, though. Why was she standing in *his* backyard? He took the stairs two at a time, but when he opened the kitchen door, the back gate was hanging open and the woman was gone. He scanned the shadows in the alleyway beyond, but there was no sign of her at all.

"You know what the agreement says, Alec." Shari twisted his name into something like a curse.

Alec swallowed hard before answering. "Would you listen to me? I don't care what your lawyer says. I don't want to only see Megan on Wednesdays and every other weekend. Christ, we live fifteen minutes from each other. She's my daughter, and I should be able to see her anytime I want. All I'm asking is for a little leeway from you."

"I said no. There's nothing more to discuss."

The phone went silent in Alec's hand. He threw it down on the sofa with a groan muffled behind a clenched jaw. Shari swore she didn't want a war, but he couldn't figure out how she thought this would turn into anything else. A rigid schedule of when he could see his own daughter? Fuck that. Fuck that hard. He was paying Shari more money than his lawyer said he had to; she could at least bend on her side a little. He wasn't asking for the moon, just more time with his daughter.

In the kitchen, he shoved the curtain aside and stared out into the backyard, scanning the dark-shrouded corners.

A week later, he woke to the crying again. The woman in blue was in the same spot, her shoulders hunched, dressed in the same dress. The waning moon offered little light, yet he could see her clearly as if she'd trapped enough to wrap her in a halo. She didn't turn around this time, simply remained in place, shedding her tears. The skin of her upper arm appeared discolored. Bruises?

The clouds slipped over the moon, turning everything into a pool of shadows; when they moved away again, the yard was empty, the gate hanging open once again.

If not for the gate, he might entertain the thought of a ghost. The house *was* old, and while Alec wasn't sure he believed in ghosts, he wasn't sure he *didn't* believe in them either.

☙   ❧

"Make a wish, Daddy."

Megan held the dandelion in one hand, gripping it tight. Around them, his neighborhood was filled with the sounds of barking dogs and laughing kids and the rhythmic drone of many lawn mowers. The back gate to his yard was latched shut, as it had been when he and Megan first stepped out into the yard.

"Maybe in a minute. Let me finish my coffee first, okay?"

She cupped her hand around the dandelion. "Dandelions are my favorite flower, but Mommy said they're a weed. That's not true, is it?"

He chuckled. "I'm afraid it is."

She squeezed her eyes half shut and pursed her lips. "Uh-*uh*. They're a flower and they're magic and if you make a wish, it has to come true."

"You are silly."

She remained quiet for several minutes, staring down at her hand, and then looked up, her eyes shadowed. "Daddy? Are me and Mommy going to come and live here with you?"

"No, punkin', remember? Daddy is going to live here, you and Mommy are going to live in the other house, and you're going to come here to visit."

"But why?"

A knot tightened in his chest, a knot of barbed wire. Harsh words pushed against his lips, but it wasn't Megan's fault, none of it was her fault, and he couldn't take it out on her. He put a smile on his face that felt like broken glass but hoped it kept his words calm. "Because Mommy and Daddy can't live together anymore."

"But if you move all your clothes back, you can."

The smile tried to shatter, but he held it in place. She bent down in the grass, plucked another dandelion free, and spun in a slow circle, the seeds spreading out like white rain.

Alec tiptoed down the stairs and stood in the entrance to the kitchen. Through the window, he could see the woman. Same dress, same posture, same tears, and again, she was illuminated in a pale glow, brighter than the moon could explain.

The front door made a slight creak when he pushed it open; he padded around the side of the house as carefully, as quietly, as he could, expecting her to be gone.

She wasn't.

The marks on her arm appeared darker—swirls of green and purple in irregular patterns. Most definitely bruises. Was she seeking temporary shelter after a storm of violence? Did this yard and this house hold something in her memory, something she couldn't get back?

He took a hesitant half-step forward, and a twig snapped beneath his heel, the tiny sound a shriek in the night silence. She didn't move, but Alec sensed a stiffening of her shoulders and spine, and he retreated until he was mostly hidden by the edge of the house.

She continued to cry but, after a time, cupped her hands over her face then extended her arms and tipped her hands. He saw teardrops slip from her palms to the ground, a rain of glistening pearls, each one distinct and separate. Impossible.

He hissed in a breath, and this time, she turned; once again, his breath gathered in his chest as if his lungs had gone on holiday. He didn't think she could see him, but he pressed closer to the house. She blinked once, slowly, and then walked to the gate with a smooth, gliding step, her dress spread out behind her, and slipped through and out.

When the ability to breathe returned, Alec knelt on one knee where she'd been. Beneath his fingers, the ground felt damp in one spot, the spot where she'd spilled her tears.

It wasn't until he returned to his bedroom that he realized her dress had made no sound moving across the grass. No sound at all.

Alec's fingers gripped the phone tight hard enough to hurt. "What do you mean I can't see her tonight? We talked about it last weekend."

"I already told you, you can't just see her whenever you want, and I told you I'd think about it, that's all. Well, I thought about it, and it isn't a good idea tonight."

"She's *my* daughter, too."

"I never said she wasn't, but she has school in the morning."

He closed his eyes. Swallowed. Pressed one hand against the heart thumping madness beneath his skin, imagining a stone instead of muscle and blood. It was better, safer, that way. His attorney told him to check his anger and keep the peace, no matter what. Be the bigger person. "Both of you being angry won't help the situation," he'd said.

"Then let her spend the night, and I'll take her to school."

Shari gave a long drawn-out sigh. "I don't want to fight about this with you."

"I didn't think we were fighting," he said through clenched teeth. "Please, let me see her for a little while."

Silence. Then the dead air of a disconnected call. Alec bit back a curse and paced back and forth in the living room. Seven steps from one wall to the other. Seven back again. Seven, a number of luck. (Like eleven, and eleven years of marriage had turned out so well, didn't they?) He stopped on the sixth step, pivoting on the ball of his foot, lurching back across the room like a drunk in search of a bottle or a zombie catching the scent of flesh. Fuck seven, eleven, and anything else remotely stinking of luck. That was for other people, not him.

Why was Shari doing this to him? To Megan? They both had a right to spend time with their daughter; they were divorcing each *other*, not their daughter.

He picked up his glass of water, the shake in his hand sending water sloshing over the top. With a grimace, he threw the glass against the brick fireplace, the shatter a bright scream in the quiet. Slivers of glass and chunks of ice tumbled to the floor; streaks of water dripped down the brick.

"Fuck, fuck, fuck."

Stop it. Stop this. Get control of yourself.

He clenched his fists hard enough to hurt,

Don't let it hurt. It will pass. It has *to pass.*

picturing the stone again, hard and unbreakable. Shari was calling all the shots, and wasn't that always the way? Damn the law and the lawyers to hell. Mothers did whatever they wanted, adding new rules as they went along, and fathers were supposed to keep their heads down and their mouths shut and play along.

Six steps (Because six meant nothing, lucky or unlucky. Six was a fucking neutral.) one way, then the other, heel-toe, heel-toe, legs stiff and awkward, arms down at his sides with his fists like a boxer's, breathing in and out, the sound too loud, too *animal*. He stopped in the middle of the room and closed his eyes, willing himself still while a muscle in his jaw twitched and twitched and twitched.

Eventually that stilled, too.

The crying. Soft, desperate. Like a lullaby of sorrow. Alec used the kitchen door, opening it slowly. The woman in blue turned, then spun around toward the gate, but not fast enough to prevent him from seeing the side of her face, swollen and awash in purple and yellow.

She left behind the open gate and another damp patch on the lawn.

"Daddy?"

"Yes, punkin'?"

"How come you don't want to see me more?"

Alec took Megan's hand in his. "Never think that. Never, okay? I wish I could see you all the time."

"So how come you don't?"

"Because when Mommies and Daddies don't live together anymore, they have to follow certain rules."

"Like in school?"

"Yes, sort of like that."

"But why are the rules like that? Why can't they change them?"

He gathered her into a hug and stared over her head toward the fireplace. A piece of broken glass glittered in the edge between the slate hearth and brick, and he glanced away fast. A momentary lapse in judgment, in control, that was all it had been.

"It's not fair," Megan said.

"No, it isn't fair at all, but it's the way things are right now, okay?"

She nodded against his chest. He closed his eyes and pictured the stone, a perfect, untouchable, unbreakable sphere.

The crying crept in through the open window along with a slight breeze. Alec put his forearm over his eyes. For hours, he'd been tossing and turning with sleep an elusive ribbon he could chase but never catch, and now *she'd* returned to serenade him with woe. As if he didn't have enough of his own. He flopped over on his stomach, buried his face in the pillow.

If she was looking for a prince on a rescue mission, she'd picked the wrong yard and the wrong man.

"I wish you could go to the beach, too, Daddy."

"It's okay, maybe we can go back, just you and me, okay?"

"Okay, Daddy. Um, Mommy says I have to go finish packing. I love you."

"I love you too, punkin'. So very much."

Alec let the phone drop from his hand. A day's notice from Shari that she was taking Megan to the beach for two weeks. One day. He exhaled sharply through his nose. Better than a phone call when they were on the road, at least. He sank down on the sofa, steepled his fingers beneath his chin, and stared at the wall while images flickered on the muted television in the corner.

Sleeping pills made his brain thick and sluggish in the morning, but even with the window open, he slept

like a stone

better than he had in weeks. Months. The pills brought vivid dreams, though, dreams of Shari dragging Megan away, of crying women, of bruises, images that lingered even after coffee, and every morning when he went out into the backyard, the gate was open. After a time, he didn't even bother to close it. What was the point?

After one last hug, Alec watched Megan run into the house, her hair bouncing bright against her shoulders. Shari followed behind without a second look in his direction; Alec didn't wait for the door to shut before he drove away.

The lamp on the end table cast a small sphere of light in the living room; the rest of the house was dark. Alec took a sip of vodka, grimaced even though the alcohol went down smooth and clean, and pushed the glass aside. He stared into the shadows, not drinking, not thinking, and when the crying began (how could he even hear it, all the windows were shut?), he fumbled for his phone. He bit back a laugh. Who exactly was he going to call? The police?

She was standing in the same place, wearing the same dress, her head bowed, weeping into her hands. The bruises on her face were even darker, a violent shade of dark and angry. For a moment, the urge to step outside, to talk to her, to ask her *why*, raced through his blood stronger than the vodka. He pulled the door open, took a half-step outside. She didn't flinch, didn't move.

His hand tightened on the door knob, and he retreated back into the house. "I can't help you," he whispered.

Shari was usually waiting at the door when he dropped Megan off; this time the door was shut and the windows curtained. He held Megan's hand as they climbed the porch steps. Shari yanked the door open wide as he lifted his hand to knock, her face caught up in a scowl.

"You're late," she said.

"We got caught in traffic, sorry."

Shari's mouth pressed into a thin line; her eyes turned steely. "Oh, I forgot, Megan can't see you this weekend. She's going on a camping trip to Rock Creek Park with school."

He nodded. "Okay."

"No, Mommy, I want to go with Daddy, not on the stupid trip, remember?"

"I understand that, honey, but I already told them you were going. You'll see Daddy the next weekend."

"But I don't want to go on the trip. Please, please, Mommy, let me go with Daddy. We're going to the big zoo to see the baby pandas."

When Shari spoke again, her voice was hard. "The zoo will still be there next weekend. Why don't you go in the house now?"

"No." Megan tugged Alec's hand. Tears spilled down her cheeks. "Daddy, tell Mommy not to make me go on the trip, please. I want to come with you instead. Please, Daddy, please."

"Mommy's right, the zoo will still be there next weekend, and so will the baby pandas." He turned away and walked back to his car. Megan would be fine. Kids cried all the time when they didn't get what they wanted.

Another night. Another room filled with the weight of silence. Outside, a light rain tapped against the windows, and thunder boomed in the distance. The living room turned to shadows and grey, and, eventually, he closed his eyes and let sleep tug him down.

He woke with a jolt, one hand pressed to his chest, the echo of thunder still in his ears. Rain pummeled the windows, obscuring everything beyond. Lightning split the sky. The lamp flickered, another boom of thunder raged in the night, and the light went out.

With his arms outstretched, he felt his way into the kitchen, fumbling in a drawer for candles and matches. He had one candle lit when he glanced out the window as another slash of lightning stripped away the dark. Oblivious to the storm, the woman was standing in the backyard, weeping.

He scrubbed his face with his hands. Was she in such a bad situation that his yard in a storm was preferable? What kind of nightmare was she trying to escape from, and why didn't she just run away for good?

Before he could change his mind, he opened the kitchen door. A gust of wind tugged it from his hand and shoved it back against the wall. He staggered out into the rain, arms over his head, feet slipping on the wet grass.

She didn't turn around, didn't acknowledge him in any way. Her entire arm was a study in violence, not only bruising but deep gashes that openly bled their red. Neither rain nor wind touched her hair, her dress. She was a small statue of calm amid the chaos, save for her weeping.

When he drew close, she turned slowly. Her left eye was blackened, her right cheek inflamed. A split in her lower lip gaped open, revealing the pink meat below. Her chin was raw as if someone had dragged her down a concrete step. Scratches and cuts, some deep, some superficial, marred the skin of her chest visible above the neckline of her dress. And still, she wept.

He let out a ragged breath. In his mind, he saw Megan's face streaked with tears, saw himself turning away, felt the sharp sting of guilt, of failure.

"Please, come inside," he shouted against the storm still drenching his clothes and hair. "You can't stay outside in this. I promise I won't hurt you."

She didn't move.

"But are you ready?" she said softly, her voice clear even through the storm's anger.

He shook his head. "For what?"

She touched his chest; in a split-second, the storm no longer touched him. He could still hear the wind, the rain, the thunder, but all were muffled as if from a great distance away. Water dripped from his arms and legs down onto the dry grass beneath his feet.

Inside his chest, he felt something tug and twist. She smiled and took his hand. Her skin was cool, but not cold. So close, her wounds were even more horrific, yet she smelled not of sweat and hurt, but flowers and time. Tears continued to slip from her eyes; as soon as one fell, another took its place, trailing a shimmering line down her cheek.

"What happened to you?" he said. "Why were you outside in the storm? Why have you been standing out here?"

She pressed a finger to his lips, and the cool kiss of her skin against his felt strange, *other*, as if she was of some elsewhere, trapped in thiswhere in a way Alec knew he'd never understand.

He reached out a hand and wiped the tears from her cheeks. "Why do you keep crying?"

She smiled. "I feel like I'm drowning," she said. "Like my chest is filled with dandelion fluff and I can't breathe through the wasted wishes."

Her voice carried a lilt, a melody.

"I don't understand," Alec said, unable to take his eyes away from hers.

"See?" She coughed, gently, delicately, and held out her hand. There, on the unlined skin of her palm, a tiny speck of white. Maybe dust, maybe his imagination.

"What is it?"

She folded her fingers over; when she released them, the white had vanished. "A wish."

"For what?"

"For happiness and joy instead of heartache and grief, for a smile instead of a tear."

"I don't understand," he said again, shaking his head. "Who, *what*, are you?"

She smiled. "I am the Algea, the three, Lupe and Ania and Achus, the daughters of Eris, the spirit of suffering of body and mind. In other lands, I have been named the Dolores, Nedolya, Cihuacoatl, but my name is of no matter. I know no torment though I carry it in my veins; I know no heartache though I taste it in my tears. I am grief and sorrow and ache, condemned to feel everything in my command, now and always." She gave a small smile. "But I think it's time. I think you're ready."

"For what?"

She leaned forward and pressed her lips to his, one quick touch that tasted of sunshine after a long rain. "For this," she whispered against his mouth. "To feel again. To feel everything."

He felt a pulling in his chest, a twinge in the back of his throat, a sense of shattering at the edges and deep below. A rush of anger flowed through his veins, pushing aside the chrysalis of numbness he'd wrapped around himself. He saw Shari's hard eyes, the document stating when he could and couldn't see his daughter, the lawyer's bill. The anger turned to rage, covering him in a wave of red, blood-dark and reeking.

The bruises on the woman's skin darkened, the cuts widened and wept ruby pearls. Runnels of red poured down her arms, changing from a flow to a trickle to nothing at all. His fault, he knew this was his fault. He tried to swallow the anger, but it was too big, too heavy to hold inside, and in spite of the blood and the bruises, she was still smiling.

"You have to feel," she whispered.

The twinge in his throat became a sob, then another. He thought of the lonely nights in this strange, quiet house, the moments he'd miss because he wasn't there, Megan's sorrow and his inability to take it away. Tears poured from his eyes, and he cupped the back of his head in his palms. Too much, it was too much. He let out a groan, wiped his face with angry swipes of his hands, and she touched his arm.

"Let it come," she said. "Let it out."

Like a tsunami, anger and hurt and loss and despair washed over him. The arguments, the harsh words, the emptiness, the changes. He shrieked into his palms even as the world turned to a blur beyond his tears; his heart broke a thousand times; his rage twisted a thousand razor-sharp coils in his gut.

A sound like tearing paper filled the air as cracks appeared in her skin. He wanted to reach for her, to find some way to save her, but the storm inside held him immobile, captive. Pieces of her began to fall, revealing a grey shadow behind them, and as each piece fell, it faded into nothing before it reached the ground.

Not decay, but disintegration, dissolution, until what stood in front of him was merely shimmering darkness in the shape of a woman; a liquid veil of night. And in the space of an eyeblink, that, too, was gone.

He exhaled long and low. Took his hands away. Hiccupped a last sob. He felt…empty but not numb, empty as if he'd been stripped of hidden chains. On the grass below, a tiny scrap of blue fabric, and atop that, one small, perfect sphere of water. He sank to his knees, reached out a fingertip, and when he touched it to his tongue, he tasted the salt of a tear. The fabric warmed the skin of his palm for a moment, then it melted away, leaving behind a dandelion seed. He closed his fingers tight and made a wish.

The sounds of the night slowly trickled back in—a breeze through branches, the drip of water from the eaves, the rhythmic clicking of crickets. The air was awash with the echo of rain, a smell of blank pages, of beginnings, and when Alec opened his hand, the seed, like the storm outside and in, was gone.

Always,
They Whisper

ↂ ↄ

She was not a monster, nor did Perseus cut off her head. The whole Athena and shield bit? Bullshit. Perseus was a self-absorbed fool who barely had the strength to lift a sword over his shoulder, let alone swing it hard enough to sever sinew and bone.

As far as the rest of her story, the snakes and stone might be true, but not in the way you think. It's always easy to paint a villain, harder to scrape below the gilt to find the real.

Medi pushes away from her desk, rubbing her eyes. Translating ancient Greek is usually a piece of cake, but for this project, she's working off photographs, not the actual documents themselves, and the faded text is nearly illegible.

She knows she should keep working, but she'd rather drink wine and watch a movie. She'll deal with the rest of the translation later.

In the kitchen, her mouth twists. Her last bottle of wine is almost empty. It's not necessary, but wants never are. She checks the mirror. There aren't quite enough wrinkles for her liking, but they should be enough.

When she unwraps the heavy towel from her head, the serpents whisper. She does her best to ignore them and puts on an ugly floral scarf and her sunglasses. Never mind that the sky is a shade of dusky purple.

Outside, she steps into the sound of bass-heavy music pumping from a car speaker and the stink of exhaust. She hates it all—the noise, the desperation—but the thought of living in a place where she can't be just another anonymous body is terrifying.

Especially for her.

Although the sidewalks are nearly deserted, she keeps her gaze down and her steps brisk. The autumn air is cool against her cheeks. Despite the wrinkles and sunglasses, her heart races the entire way.

The man at the liquor store takes her money without a word. He gave up trying to engage her in conversation a long time ago.

On her way back to her apartment, the screech of tires fills the air. A door opens and closes behind her. Then she hears the steady thump of shoes on pavement. She glances over her shoulder, and when she turns back, a man is standing close. Too close. She tries to dodge out of the way, hits his arm instead, and stumbles. He grabs for her, her sunglasses tilt, and she doesn't look away fast enough. Keeping her guard up is hard, even after all her years of practice.

But he isn't looking at her face, her eyes. Relief flows through her body. She nudges her glasses back into their proper position and says, "Thank you."

"No problem. Be careful, okay?" he says in a solicitous manner.

Her heart is still pounding heavy in her chest when she slams and locks her front door. Half a glass of wine downed in two gulps eases it somewhat. She feels the weight of the serpents hidden inside the spiral curls of her hair. She muffles their words with a towel again.

No mortal can understand what they say. Athena granted that mercy at least.

How many times do you have to hear something before you believe it to be true?

Not nearly as many as you think.

Every Sunday morning, Medi wakes early, regardless of how late she stayed up the night before. She wraps a towel around her head and prays, but not to the gods and goddesses of her youth. They were never friends. Never a comfort.

She prays for forgiveness, for compassion, for safety. She suspects she would've had an answer by now if anyone was listening.

Then she takes a glass vial from atop her chest of drawers. The liquid inside shimmers a pale pink. When she removes the stopper, the room fills with the smell of gardenias, but it's a lie. The elixir tastes like rotten fruit and spoiled meat.

Fitting, she thinks.

There are only a few drops left in this bottle, but she only needs one, and the results last for a week, give or take a few days.

The elixir is cool on her tongue. For a long moment, there is nothing but the sound of her breathing and the muted whispers from beneath the towel. Then a slow pain burns beneath her skin, rippling out like a sheet shaken over a bed. The first time, she writhed on the floor until it was finished, but she's used to it now. Pain is part of being a woman.

When the hurt subsides and her fists unclench, she checks the mirror in the bathroom and nods at her reflection. An ugly woman stares back. A woman not worth anyone's time.

Or anyone's attention.

They have names for women like her, or maybe she's the reason for the names. Everyone needs a scapegoat.

In the old days, there was a ritual called the pharmakos. In times of drought or other hardship, a slave or an animal was driven from the city in the hope that casting out the scapegoat would also cast out the hardship.

They never formally pushed her out. They didn't have to. The words and whispers did it for them. And even though the serpents were hissing their poison, even though she fought tears the entire way, she held her head up high as she left.

There was no such shame for Poseidon.

The edge of the sky is just beginning to lighten when she finishes up the last line of translation. She sends it via email and sits back in her chair with her hands clasped behind her head. The serpents coil around her fingers. She shakes them free and puts on her scarf and sunglasses. Her clothing is already shapeless, but she grabs a cane to complete the look.

One walk around the block to clear her head and get her blood flowing is all she needs before breakfast and bed. She doesn't normally pull all-nighters, but this was a rush job. Nothing ancient this time, just a bit of modern Greek in a legal document for a writer and her literary agent. A fairly easy, well-paying assignment.

The streets are still awash in shadow. Her cane thumps against the pavement. She doesn't hunch over or force her feet into a slow and halting rhythm; there's no one around to see. She drops a few dollars into a homeless man's cup. He's snoring loudly, oblivious to her presence, and she hopes he wakes before someone else steals the money.

As she withdraws her hand, she sees smooth skin and frowns. She pats her cheek. Her frown turns into a gaping hole of shock. No, it isn't possible. It's only been two days.

At her feet, the man shifts. Mumbles. She turns and runs the rest of the way home. Inside, she drops the cane, rips the sunglasses and scarf free, tosses them onto the floor, and races into her bathroom. The bright lights reveal an absence of wrinkles. In their place, smooth skin, a firm jawline. A young woman's face, although she's anything but. The part in the old stories about her mortality?

Wrong.

They also like to portray her as a hag or a monster. She's never been either one naturally, and if she were, would so many have tried to claim and conquer her?

She grips the edge of the porcelain. Stares down at the white as she fights the tears. The serpents twitch awake, then settle back to sleep without a sound. She's grateful; she doesn't need their input right now. Her breath comes fast, and her fingers tremble.

Maybe the last few drops spoiled somehow. A logical, legitimate reason. She'll toss out the remaining elixir and make a new batch.

From the tiny herb garden in her kitchen, she snips two amaratho leaves, for courage and longevity, tugs a few anithos seeds free, for protection, and slices off a bit of daphni, for purification. She grinds them together with a mortar and pestle until her wrist aches, switches hands, and keeps working until the mixture is fine.

Using a small funnel, she pours the powder into the vial and adds purified water infused with lygos. A poetic bit of irony; in days of old, it was used to calm sexual appetites. Finally, she adds three drops of an oil nicknamed *Tears of the Lonely.*

She pours the elixir into a vial and shakes it until everything blends. It took her years to get the mixture just right, but now she could make it in her sleep.

It needs to sit for twenty-four hours before she can take it. Luckily, she doesn't have anywhere to go, and her apartment walls are safe. Inside, she doesn't need her disguise.

She doesn't bother with a towel on her head. She doesn't pray. Just drops the elixir on her tongue. She welcomes the pain that rushes in, just as she welcomes the hag in the mirror when it's done.

She breathes heavily, relieved enough to ignore the serpents and the words they whisper.

But the next morning, the hag is gone. The woman in the bathroom is young. Beautiful. A face she knows. A face she hates.

She stands in front of the bathroom mirror, one hand on her cheek, unable to move, unable to think. It's not possible.

A serpent slips free from the towel. Breathes on her cheek. Whispers.

Your fault.

The spell breaks, and she backs away from the mirror with her hands covering her ears.

"Stop it, stop it, stop it."

Of course it was her fault. She must not have used enough. She shoves the serpent back beneath the towel and races into her bedroom. Another drop of elixir. Another welcome bite of pain. Another mask of age spots and wrinkles.

Beneath the towel, the serpents stir.

Once again, the hag is gone come morning.

Perseus came to her the week before she left. He reached for her cheek and said nothing when she pulled away. Then he offered marriage. She laughed, thinking it a joke.

It wasn't.

Never mind that he had a half-dozen other women fawning all over him, including Athena. Any one of them would've jumped at the chance to be his wife. He was good looking—Medi had to give him that—but he knew it and never let anyone forget it.

The hesitant smile on his face vanished. His jaw clenched. She tried to explain the why, but he wasn't interested, and with each word from her lips, his anger grew. No, it was more than anger. It was rage. And his parting words?

"As if anyone else would ever want you now."

Medi's hand shakes as she removes the stopper from the vial, but after the drop touches her tongue, there is no pain. No change. She bites back a sob.

In the kitchen, she checks all the plants. No signs of rot or infestation of any kind. The water infusion smells fine, as does the oil. Tears slip from her eyes as she makes another batch. She knows she didn't make any mistakes before. She knows it as sure as she knows her own name.

Still, she grinds the herbs until her fingers are numb from the effort.

Twenty-four hours later, Medi perches on the edge of her sofa, the vial on the coffee table. The museum sent an email, requesting that she come in to look at some recently discovered documents. She asked for photographs, but they were beyond illegible.

She picks up the vial. If she wants this assignment, she'll have to go, and she needs the money. She pulls the stopper free.

"Please work. Please, please work."

One drop on her tongue.

Nothing happens.

Another drop.

Still nothing.

She drains the contents. Pain rips through her belly, but she doesn't feel her skin change, and when she holds out one hand, the flesh is still smooth.

"No, no, no!"

She hurls the vial across the room. Shards of glass rain down on the floor when it shatters against the wall. She shrieks into her palms.

She can't go to the museum. She can't go anywhere at all.

She gets up, wipes the tears from her cheeks with angry swipes of the back of her hand, and stalks into the kitchen. Pulls out the herbs, the water, the oil. Grinds and pours and mixes and waits.

It doesn't work.

She buries her face in a pillow so the neighbors won't hear her cries.

ಶ಼಼   ಶ಼

As she crawled away from Poseidon, with tears on her face, blood on her thighs, and bruises on her arms, she saw Athena standing near the temple entrance, her arms crossed over her chest. Medi whispered, and to this day she cannot remember what she said. "Help," or perhaps she simply said Athena's name.

But she will never forget the words that spilled from Athena's mouth. Never. The serpents remind her every single day.

She ignores the museum's emails. Their phone calls. She paces; the serpents slip and slither through her curls. She feels their breath on her cheeks; knows the whispers aren't far behind.

(Would that Athena had cursed her with the true face of a hag instead of this, but that would have been a kindness. And that wasn't Athena's style.)

She takes a deep breath. And another. Everything will be fine. It *will*. She won't panic. She grabs her sunglasses and stands at the door for a long time. How long has it been since she went out into the world with her real face exposed on purpose? Years— many, many years.

I can do this, she thinks.

She has to. A quick trip to the shop for fresh herbs and oil. Maybe she can experiment with the mixture a bit. After so many years, perhaps she's built up a tolerance and now she needs to add something else.

She puts her hand on the doorknob. Maybe it won't be so bad. Takes her hand away. Maybe she shouldn't go out. Does she really have to go? But if not, then what?

Maybe she should order what she needs online and pay for overnight shipping; then she won't—

Stop it!

"I can do this," she whispers, tugging her scarf tighter.

Between the scarf, the sunglasses, the shapeless clothes, it has to be safe. The shop is only a few blocks away. Her heart races as she steps outside.

At the end of the street, she passes a group of men. They're speaking loudly. Laughing. She doesn't like the edge of their laughter. It's hard. Like a fist, like the words bitch and cunt. Her back goes straight, her mouth dry.

The serpents stir. She takes a deep breath. Walks past with eyes down. *Don't look at me, don't look at me,* she thinks, but she feels their gazes crawling all over her back as if she were wearing nothing more than stiletto heels and a smile.

But they don't follow. They don't say a word. She turns the corner. Passes a woman in a business suit who gives her a quick nod. Another woman, younger, this one busy with her cell phone. Then a man emerges from a doorway, but he passes by without looking as well. She allows herself a small smile. Not much farther now.

She turns the last corner and runs into someone. A man. Hard enough to send her sunglasses flying to the ground. She drops her eyes, but it's too late. His eyes are wide. Dark. Fixed on hers for only a second, but it's a second too long, and he's smitten. Yes, the first part of the curse happens that fast. Her heart races madness. He reaches for her arm; she pulls away.

"Hi," he says with a smile.

She says nothing. Takes a step back, pulling her arm away, and bends down, her fingers scrabbling on the pavement for her glasses. He bends down, too. His hands reach the glasses first.

"Here, let me help," he says.

She shakes her head. Steps to the side. He does the same.

"It's a beautiful day, isn't it?"

She steps again. As does he. Can't he see the frumpy dress? The heavy-soled shoes, for the gods' sake? (But of course, it's too late for the camouflage. He saw her face. He looked into her eyes.)

"Please, let me pass," she says.

"Why don't you stay, and we can talk for a while?"

She shakes her head again.

"So what, you won't talk to me?"

She takes a step back, away from the edge in his voice.

He steps forward. Grabs her arm, his fingers digging in hard.

"Why do you have to act that way?" he says. "I just want to talk to you."

She looks up. It doesn't matter now anyway. She sees the stone set of his eyes—the second part of the curse. All the breath rushes from her lungs. The serpents shiver.

"Please leave me alone."

"Please leave me alone," he repeats in a sing-song voice.

She turns. Breaks into a run. Hears a name (one of *those* names) carried on the breeze and quickens her steps before it can echo in her ears.

The serpents wake. *See what happens?* they say. *See what you make happen?*

"Stop it," she whispers. "Please."

Your fault.

She locks her apartment door behind her and covers her ears, but still, the serpents whisper sharp-barbed reminders she doesn't need; she knows all too well where the blame falls. Where it's always fallen.

All your fault. You shouldn't have smiled at Poseidon. You shouldn't have been there.

She curls up in a ball on the floor, praying the serpents will fall to silence, but of course they don't.

Poseidon said he wanted to talk. He lied.

"It's not my fault you're so beautiful," he said.

But what about when she begged him to stop? When he pressed his hand over her mouth to hold in her screams? When he ripped open her tunic?

After, she went into seclusion. It was for the best. A few months later, when she braved the world again, her eyes, her face, safely hidden behind a veil, she heard the first whispers.

Serpentine and human both.

The intercom buzzes. A moment later, a gruff voice says, "Delivery."

"Leave it at the door," Medi calls out.

When the footsteps retreat, she brings the box inside and slices open the tape. The serpents press against her scalp as she crushes and grinds and blends, holding tight to hope.

She sits on the floor in the corner of her kitchen, amid a scatter of leaves and berries and drops of oil. Nothing has worked. Nothing. She rests her face in her hands, her shoulders slumped.

The curse has won. *They* have won.

Silent tears slip between her fingers. Doesn't she deserve peace after all this time? Hasn't she paid enough for Poseidon's lust?

One serpent curls around her ear. *Your fault*, it whispers softly.

But why? What has she ever done but exist?

She rocks back and forth while the serpents whisper again and again. The towel can only muffle so much.

Once upon a time, she was a young girl, a priestess in Athena's temple who wanted nothing more than to wake each morning with the sun, to assist with the rituals, to drink from the sacred spring.

Medi tosses and turns beneath the sheets. In the darkness, she remembers the weight of an unwanted body against hers, a mouth pressed hard against lips fighting to scream, wrists straining beneath the iron grip of a hand as the ugliness, the guilt, spilled out of him and into her, marking her as sure as a brand.

Pariah. Anathema.

She chokes back a moan, pushing hard on the scarf wrapped tightly around her head, but even so, she can hear the serpents' reminder of the how and the why. She sits up, gasping for air, drowning in waves so high, so violent, she's sure they'll pull her under.

On trembling legs, she staggers into the bathroom and stares at her reflection, her eyes filled with hate. She opens the medicine cabinet, and there on the shelf, a straight razor waits.

Will this make them happy?

She grips the handle tight, the blade glimmering in the overhead light, and touches it to the delicate skin of her wrist. The blue veins beneath her flesh point the way like tiny lines on a map leading to an exit ramp.

A serpent slips from beneath the scarf. Coils. Uncoils. Its tongue flickers cool against her temple.

Your fault, it whispers.

She presses the blade. A tiny wound opens. A single pearl of red runs free.

Your fault.

This is the only way to make them stop, isn't it? She watches the red run across the pale of her skin, drop to the sink, and slide down the porcelain into the waiting mouth of the drain.

Her lip curls. Hasn't she bled enough? Hasn't she given up enough? She rips the scarf from her head, grabs a serpent, and forces its maw open. It hisses and writhes in her fist.

Your fault.

"Shut up, shut up, shut up."

She cuts out the serpent's tongue. The pain is like a fire raging unchecked beneath her scalp, a thousand brutal words slamming against her skin. The blade slips from her hands, and she covers her mouth to hold in the scream.

The tongue sits in the basin, dark against the white. Like an exclamation point. Like an accusation.

She takes her hands away. Shrieks. Grabs another serpent. Grabs the blade.

"Not my fault."

Another tongue falls. She reaches for another serpent.

"Not my fault."

Again, the blade. Again, the pain.

"It was *never* my fault."

One by one, the tongues fall, and when the last is gone, she drops the razor on the floor. The serpents are writhing, their hateful words now the sibilance of rage, of warning, of something else she cannot define, though it feels right and sure.

The pain slowly fades to a dull ache. Perhaps it will remain, perhaps time will turn it to memory, but it doesn't matter. She stands tall. Smiles. Brushes her hair away from her face. Her eyes are full of tears—a sign of the pain or of triumph or perhaps a little of both. Her skin is still smooth; her face still a maiden's. If the visage captures a man's fancy, if it turns his heart to stone, so be it. She will not apologize for who, for what, she is anymore. It's time to reveal the truth and rewrite the story, her story, the way it was meant to be written all along.

Once upon a time, she wasn't the villain.

Dysphonia in
D Minor

ରେ ଐ

I. FRAME

We sang our first bridge, a marvel of twisted cables and soaring towers, when Lucia's hair was long and I thought love was a promise of always. It wasn't our best or our strongest, but it was the first and had passion and hope as its support. Because we were foolish, we thought it would last forever, but first songs never lasted that long, no matter how much power the notes held in the making.

We knew our testing would change things, no matter what we said otherwise. Builders did best on their own, especially if their Voice was powerful. We always thought mine would be the strong one.

But we were young.

II. BEAM

"Where are they sending you?" I whispered in Lucia's ear, the night before she was scheduled to leave on her first assignment.

The chirrup of bugs and the scent of white lilies wafted in through the open window. The curtains fluttered in the breeze, revealing a hint of the darkness beyond.

When Lucia rolled on her side, her hair fell over her shoulder in a riot of spiral curls. She took my hand, and our fingers intertwined. Her brow creased. "You know I can't tell you."

"I won't tell anyone."

"Delanna, I know you're upset because I'm going, but please, let it go. I can't tell you."

She started to rise from the bed. I put my hand on her arm.

"I'm not upset," I whispered. "I'm just going to miss you."

"I'll miss you, too."

I rolled over and grabbed my glass of wine. "Are you sure you don't want some?"

She sighed. "You know I can't do that, either."

I should not have offered; I knew she couldn't. No cigarettes, no alcohol, no acidic foods. And the musts: a tablespoon of honey three times a day, a scarf wrapped round her neck, no matter the temperature, and a willingness to stay silent.

"Maybe they should keep you in a gilded cage." My words came out sharper than I intended. Warmth bloomed under my cheeks.

"That isn't fair," she said.

"Okay, I'm sorry." I traced my fingertips along her cheekbones, her jaw, the tiny dimple in the center of her chin, the fullness of her lower lip. "Please, I'm sorry."

She took my hands away and shook her head. "I have to go. I'll come and see you as soon as I get back, and if I can call you while I'm there, I will."

The old stories said the first Voice belonged to a girl who emerged from a whirlwind storm. The storm's origin, land or water, depended on the teller of the tale. The girl's name, the same. My mother said the how didn't matter and some mysteries were best kept that way.

There were still buildings in the oldest section of the capitol city said to be her creations, towering things of arches and alcoves, rooms that swallowed up every sound, every heartbeat. When I was small, I tried to chip away a piece of stone from one—for what purpose, I can only guess—and my mother smacked my hand hard enough to leave a mark of her anger behind.

Lucia didn't call.

I saw her creation on television—a new dam crafted of pale white stone streaked with grey in a country on the opposite side of the world. I knew it was hers; I could almost hear her notes, her perfection.

My chest ached, and my eyes burned with tears. I buried my face in a sweater she'd left behind and breathed in her scent, willing her to come home soon.

Until a few years ago, our builders never sang on foreign soil. Now, though, there were churches and museums and monuments across the world shaped by our Voices.

Some said our gift came from the goddesses below the surrounding sea, while others claimed a magic in the air. Still others said Voice was the reason our tiny country had never seen war upon its shores, that no one wanted to taint the beauty of our land or the gift in our blood with hatred and weaponry. Perhaps they were afraid of what other talents we might have hidden. Tourists came to see what we'd built but were never allowed to hear the making.

I wondered if they'd altered the rules; I wondered if they'd allowed anyone to hear Lucia's Voice. A bitter taste filled my mouth, stronger than the taste of tears.

"I can feel it inside you," she said to me one night when we were half-asleep in tangled sheets.

"What? My heart?" I said with a laugh.

"No, your Voice." She placed one hand between my breasts. "It's here."

I laughed in the darkness. So did she. Then we kissed, and all thoughts of Voice disappeared into urgent whispers and the soft sounds of love.

The testing was only a few months away. We still thought we had forever.

A river ran along the back of my family's expansive property. I don't know when the tradition started, but a bridge sung by my mother stood not far from one crafted by my grandmother. Traces of older bridges, older attempts, lingered here and there as rubble on the shore, nothing more. Even the best Builders made mistakes sometimes. Especially in the beginning. Love tokens, my mother called them. Even the broken ones.

"You will understand when you're older," she'd said.

She was right.

A night after her testing and a month before mine, Lucia woke me in the early hours of the morning.

"Come with me," she said.

We ran in our nightgowns to the river with our hands linked together, shivering in the chill air. We kissed on the shore, then she jumped in the water and swam across to the other side. She emerged from the river dripping wet, her hair plastered to her shoulders and back.

"Sing with me," she called out.

When her Voice filled the night air, tears spilled down my cheeks. It was pure and true and beautiful. No mere song, but a symphony. After her testing, they told her she had the strongest Voice they'd heard in decades. Anyone who heard her sing would believe it.

It didn't take long for her creation to take shape. I added my Voice to hers. Our notes mingled and danced and built. When it was finished, she walked back across the bridge, her feet whispering on the stone, and we held each other close.

"We'll travel the world and build together, but this, this will always be ours," she said.

I cupped her face in my hands and spoke against her mouth, her lips warm beneath mine. "Always."

We made love on the shore with our bridge soaring overhead and stars in our eyes.

III. SPAN

Three months after the dam was unveiled, she showed up on my doorstep with flowers in her hand. I ran into her arms.

"Why didn't you tell me you were coming home? I would've made dinner. I would've—"

She pressed one hand to my lips.

I kissed her palm and spoke against her skin, my words muffled. "How long are you home?"

"Not very long," she said.

"I've missed you so much."

Later, in the dark, I said, "I saw the dam."

"You know I can't talk about that."

I rolled my eyes. Such an absurd rule. Who would hear anyway? The walls, the pillows? I wouldn't run out and tell the world; I thought Lucia knew me better than that. I didn't understand the need for secrecy. We never had to keep secrets when we built at home, even those who built for the government.

"What's it like?"

There was a long silence, then a smile playdanced across her face.

"It's amazing, but it's hard, harder than I thought it would be."

"That's it? Amazing? Hard?"

She shook her head. "What do you want me to say?"

"How does it feel, inside?"

"Like I've opened a door and all the notes come flooding out. It's beautiful and scary and. . ." She gave a small shake of her head again. "It's hard to describe it so you'd understand."

"Because I don't know anything about Voice."

"Don't say it like that."

"What?"

"It's not my fault."

"I didn't say it was."

"Not with your mouth, no. I don't want to fight with you."

She was gone again when I woke.

Our second bridge was delicate and fragile with carved waist-high railings. It was crooked in the middle. My fault. I'd had too much wine.

We loved it anyway.

Six months later, I woke up to find her asleep beside me. Her hair was cut close to her scalp. I traced the contours of her face until she woke.

"I miss your hair," I said, "but I miss you more."

I pretended not to notice that she didn't say she missed me, too. I didn't ask her about what she'd built, and she didn't offer. It was better, safer, that way.

But we built another bridge before she left, a beautiful structure that gleamed silver-pale in the moonlight.

Testing wasn't mandatory. Many people built for pleasure, not profit. There were no laws against building for personal use. My family was one of the oldest and wealthiest in the country, and neither my mother nor her mother chose to test, but my heart wanted a different path. I wanted to mean something. To matter.

Maybe I'd always wanted too much.

Afterward, with my chest heavy with failure, I went to her apartment. She knew the minute she saw my face. When my tears stopped, she wiped my face and kissed my forehead.

"They detected notes of discordance," I said, my voice thick. "It makes my Voice unstable. Worthless."

"I'm sorry," she whispered into my hair. "I'm so, so sorry."

She took my hand and led me to the river.

"Sing," she said.

"I can't."

"Yes, you can. No matter what they said." She squeezed my hand hard. "And you know you can. You've built plenty of things before."

I tried. I did. But my Voice emerged broken and pale. The stone crumbled. The girders warped. I put my head in my hands and wept again.

I didn't understand. Had my Voice changed? Had the testing revealed a truth I'd never wanted to see? Was *I* broken?

Nine months went without a word. I caught sight of her on the news. Never her face or form, only what she'd built. A statue of another country's goddess, a museum that would soon be filled with the treasures from an archaeological dig, and so many others. They were all so beautiful. So perfect.

I was proud of her, proud of her Voice, or so I told myself in the quiet hours after waking with the memory of her touch still on my skin.

Then I bumped into her at a coffee shop.

"Lucia?"

She turned slowly, too slowly, her face curiously devoid of emotion. She offered a smile, but it didn't reach her eyes.

"When did you get back?" I asked.

"Yesterday, but I'm leaving early in the morning."

I wiped the hurt from my face, but I knew she saw it.

"So soon?"

"Yes."

The word came out sharp enough to sting.

I convinced her to come to my house. We made love. When she kissed me, her mouth was hard, and her fingers left tiny marks on my skin. A punishment, perhaps. But for what?

We said I love you; we didn't say goodbye. But I tasted the truth in her lips, hidden beneath a cold chill.

In the morning, I found a new bridge across the river. It was beautiful, all shimmering cables and delicate scrollwork. I hated it on sight.

IV. ARCH

The news broke the story of a new prison in a country I'd never heard of, and when I recognized its shape, I turned off the television with a snarl. The Lucia I once knew would have refused.

And why didn't she leave? Contracts, like hearts, could be broken. I waited for a call. A letter. Anything at all. I wanted to hear her say it was over. I deserved that much.

Standing by the river, I sang broken bits of stone and cables that untwisted as soon as they were made. My Voice was only strong when it was entwined with hers.

I poured over satellite imagery and found traces of her in a sweatshop, a brothel, another prison. Pretty things that could not hide the ugliness of their intent.

Did she want to build such things? Had she been building them all along, even when the news showed the statues and museums? Did they force her?

I hated her.

I hated that I still loved her.

Strangers with long hair and laughing eyes filled my bed. I drank wine and vodka. Smoked cigarettes. Ate chips with vinegar. Turned on the music and sang with my regular voice until it was hoarse. Screamed until I couldn't speak. Exposed myself to anyone with a cough or a labored breath. Spent weeks with inflamed tonsils and a fever.

I visited all the places she'd loved to go, hoping for a glimpse of her face, yet dreading the same. No matter how hard I tried, I could not forget the scent of her hair, the way her body felt next to mine, the way her lips always tasted of honey.

Our third bridge was narrow with no railings, just a shining sheet of marble that spanned the river. We sang our initials into the stone, stood at its apex, and made a wish on a shooting star.

I saw her in the city square the day of the spring festival, half-hidden by the crowd. She was standing with her arms crossed, staring at the buildings built by others a long time ago. I saw a hard glint in her eyes and a strange twist on her mouth. A ghost of someone I once knew.

With a heart full of broken hope, I called out her name. Her head turned in my direction, our gazes caught and held for one quick moment, then she vanished into the crowd.

I ran to the space where she'd been and thought I saw her again, but when I called her name the second time, she didn't turn around.

Maybe she hadn't seen me.

I almost believed it.

When I saw a palace built in a country known for its subjugation of women, I unplugged my television. A light rain was falling as I walked to the river with my hands clenched into fists. How could she? Why would she?

I recalled the distant, dismissive look in her eyes. That wasn't my Lucia. She wasn't hard. She didn't hurt.

But maybe I'd only seen what I wanted to. Maybe I always had.

Our bridges stood like silent soldiers. I took a deep breath and sang discordance. Destruction. The night air filled with the high-pitched screech of metal on metal, the twang of sprung cables, and heavy thuds. Steel curled away in ribbons from the framework. The cables tied and twisted into complicated knots. The sheet of marble crumbled into pebbles to line the river bottom.

I left the first bridge alone. It didn't need my Voice. Time would take its own toll. My tears tasted of honey, of loss, yet buried deep within, a hint of steel and stone. Of strength. And when my sorrow dried to salt upon my cheeks, I walked away and left behind all the pieces I'd unmade.

I slept with a records man in the government office in exchange for information. The stubble on his cheeks left red marks on my breasts, and afterward, I stood in the shower until the water turned to ice, trying to erase the feel of his weight from my body.

I plugged my television back in and watched countless hours of plastic-faced newscasters. Every time I closed my eyes, I saw the look on Lucia's face. Felt the empty space in the bed. Felt my hands become fists and my chest tighten.

I packed my suitcase.

No grand ceremonies had been held to celebrate the camps Lucia built high in the mountains in a country with a sordid history. I read documents that stated the camps were to help with prison overcrowding, but I didn't believe them. New monsters often wore old monsters' faces.

They were no guards, no prisoners. Yet. I touched my hands to the outside wall and felt Lucia's song buried deep within. Why employ Lucia, why call for her talent, her beauty? Did they need it built quickly, or did they want the discretion? I took a deep breath and sang my destruction. I kept my Voice low, but my notes were steady and sure. They rose and fell and crept inside, hiding within hers.

If the government found out what I could do, I would be quietly removed or perhaps put into service destroying on command, like a trained puppy.

Would I become a story? Once upon a time, there was a woman who sang of hurt and broken things. Who tried to fix her heart by shattering the one who tore it to pieces. It didn't seem like the sort of story that came with a happy ending.

I walked away before the stone collapsed, but I heard its echo. I swallowed my guilt. I'd have more than enough before it was over.

The news said nothing. What she built, I destroyed. Out of love? Out of anger? For justice? Did it matter? I watched a thousand stones crumble, a hundred walls collapse. I waited for someone to discover what I'd done. I waited for someone to discover what I was.

It was too easy. No one ever noticed the lone figure slipping in and out of the shadows. Surely if what I'd done was wrong, someone would have.

At night, alone in strange beds in one hotel after another, I closed my eyes. Saw the look in her face. Would she smile now? Would she hate me?

Would the hurt fade away?

And then I was done.

V. SUSPENSION

On a warm day in April, I stepped outside to check the mail, and Lucia was sitting on the porch with a wine bottle in hand, no scarf around her neck. My lips parted, but only silence emerged.

"They terminated my contract," she said, her voice husky. "Vocal instability."

I kept my face still. "I'm sorry."

Her face no longer wore a stranger's expression, but there were shadows beneath her eyes and hollows under her cheekbones.

She lifted the bottle of wine. "Do you have any plans for dinner?"

Her voice wavered. I wanted to tell her no. I wanted to tell her too much time had passed and I had too many secrets, but instead, I wrapped my arms around her. I'd destroyed enough.

We talked about life. We didn't talk about bridges or Voice or building. We drank the wine and laughed and pretended the laughter wasn't strained. I searched her eyes for a sign that I'd saved her. Instead, I saw my own guilt looking back.

Later, when the sun set, I asked if she wanted to stay. She put her arms around me, but like old spoons in a drawer, our shine was tarnished, our hollows empty.

She didn't look back when she left. I wanted to call out, to tell her the truth, to beg her forgiveness, but my mouth would not make the words. I watched her disappear into the darkness until tears turned the world to a blur.

We should have ended on a different note, a fading trill in a minor chord, perhaps. Something more than silence. But for all we built and destroyed, neither one of us had the voice for goodbye.

Shall I Whisper to You of Moonlight, of Sorrow, of Pieces of Us?

ॐ ॐ

Inside each grief is a lonely ghost of silence, and inside each silence are the words we didn't say.

I find the first photograph face down on the mat outside the front door. In a rush to get to the office, I tuck it in the pocket of my trousers, thinking it a note from a neighbor. An invitation to dinner maybe.

I pull my car onto the highway, into a mess of brake lights and angry horns, and shake my head. Morning traffic is always the same. Not sure how anyone could expect otherwise.

When I reach for my cigarettes, I pull out the photo instead—you, with a lock of your hair curling over one cheek, the trace of a smile on your lips, and your eyes twin pools of dark, a touch of whimsy hidden in their depths. Beautiful. Perfect. A spray of roses peeks over your shoulder, the blooms a pale shade of ivory. Far in the distance, a faint strain of music, your favorite song, echoes away.

The surface of the photo is slick beneath my fingertips, and when I lift it to my nose I catch a hint of perfume. Sweet and delicate, but with an undertone of some exotic spice. I will never forget that smell.

I close my eyes tight against the tears. Yes, tears, even after all this time. I knew you'd find me. I've always known.

Please let me go. Please.
Never.

In the middle of the night I wake to the smell of flowers. I move from room to room with a dry mouth and a heart racing madness, turn on all the lights, and check the windows and doors. Locked or unlocked, it doesn't matter. If you want to come back, they won't stop you. Nothing will. The photographs are proof of that. Still, the locks are a routine that makes me feel as if I'm doing something other than waiting.

I peer through the glass to the backyard where moonlight is skittering across the grass. The tree branches sway gently back and forth like a couple lost in the rhythm of a dance. I whisper your name, my voice breaking, and only house noise answers. I rake my fingers through my hair. I don't know if I can go through this again, but I also know I have no choice.

I never did.

The next photo appears face up on the coffee table in the living room. Same smile, but with your hair pulled back in a ponytail. A thin chain of silver circles your neck; the fingertips of your right hand are barely touching the small medallion hanging below the hollow at the base of your throat. A trace of dark shadows the skin beneath your eyes.

Baby, those shadows say.

Yes, I still remember the sound of your voice.

I fumble a cigarette free from the pack; it takes three tries before I can hold my lighter still enough to guide the flame where it needs to go.

When my job transferred me from one coast to another, I thought the distance would be too great for you. Even when I still lived in the old house, it had been over a year since you left the last photo. I'd thought you were gone.

I know it won't be any different this time, no matter how much I want otherwise. This hope is a strange thing, a wish wrapped in barbed wire. Or maybe delusion.

The smell of flowers again in the middle of the night. I stay in bed, the sheet fisted in my hands. Heart full of chaos; head full of images.

My coworker catches me at the end of the day when I'm slipping into my coat. "Hey, a bunch of us are going to happy hour. Want to come?"

"No, maybe next time."

He raises his eyebrows and shakes his head. "That's what you said the last time."

"Sorry, I already have plans."

"You said that, too."

I shrug one shoulder, step away before he can say anything else.

I sit with the television on mute, listening to the silence. A book sits unread on the sofa beside me; a glass of iced tea long gone warm rests on the table. Condensation beads around the base of the glass like tears.

The minutes tick by. The hours pass. I listen to nothing. I wait.

Another photograph. On the bottom step of the staircase this time. You, captured on a blue and white striped blanket, shielding your eyes from the sun. Even in the frozen bright, the shadows under your eyes are visible, and your skin is too pale. Next to you on the blanket is a crumpled napkin, a plastic cup on its side, a bit of cellophane wrap holding a rainbow's arc on its surface, a few grains of sand. I hear the rush of a wave as it touches the shore, then another as it recedes. The salt tang of the ocean hovers in the air, but only for an instant.

I smell flowers in the night. Maybe it's my imagination, but the scent is growing stronger. A promise or recrimination?

The landing at the top of the stairs. The next photo. Your face half in shadow, half in light. The almost-smile is still there in spite of the pallor of your skin, the hollows beneath your cheekbones, the scarf wrapped round your head. I hear the last breath of a laugh. Smell honeysuckle drifting on a cool breeze.

Always the same photographs in the same order. I don't know how, but the how doesn't matter. And I already know the why.

(*Please let me go.*

Never.)

It will be the last photo, just like the last time. I know it will, but I check the locks anyway. Everything is as it should be. It's too cold to leave the windows open or I would.

A throat clears. I look up to see my boss standing in my office, a small frown on his face. "Are you okay?"

"Yes," I say. "Why?"

"You look a little tired, that's all."

"Just a bout of insomnia," I say. The lie slips easily from my tongue.

"You have my sympathies. My wife's had that for years. Try a glass of wine before bed. That helps her."

"Will do."

He lingers for a few moments longer, and for one quick instant, I think of telling him everything. I tried that once with your sister; she told me I should talk to a doctor, and then she stopped answering my calls.

I unlock the windows, as always, but my hand remains on the lever. I am so tired of waiting. I'm wearing shadows under my eyes now, and I have a knot in my chest that won't go away. Maybe I could learn to forget about you. To move on. Throw away the photographs, let time fade the memories. Lock the doors and the windows instead of unlocking them. Go out with my coworkers. And maybe you'll stop.

I flip the lock, sigh, and turn it back. No, I want you to come back. It's what I've always wanted. Maybe that small sliver of doubt is the reason you haven't yet.

I find a photo in the hallway just outside the bedroom door and sit with my back against the wall. I've never seen this photo before; you've never made it this close.

The smile is no longer a smile, but a grimace. The shadows beneath your eyes are now bruises of dark. I taste the bright sting of antiseptic. Hear the ticking of a clock winding down and down and down.

"Please, baby, please," I whisper, my voice hollow.

I take that tiny trace of doubt and shove it away. Hold the photo to my chest. This time will be different. I know it will.

I toss and turn for hours, listening to the quiet. The distance between the hallway and the bed seems so small, yet miles, worlds, apart as well.

Please, baby. Please.

The last words you said to me.

The next door neighbor is outside watering her plants when I get home. She waves. Smiles. I return the gesture, but not the expression. When she starts to head in my direction, I hightail it into the house. Rude, I know, but she caught me when I first moved here and kept me outside for an hour, her voice flitting from topic to topic like a bee on a mission for nectar. She doesn't pick up on any of the signs that I want to be left alone, or maybe she does and just chooses to ignore them. The way she ignores the ring on my finger.

Another photo, left on the foot of our bed. It shows only clasped hands. Matching silver bands. Fingers entwined. One hand is hale and hearty; the other frail, the veins standing out like mounds in a field of fresh graves. I feel the paper skin beneath my palm. I hear a whisper of words, promising lies, promising everything. I taste a kiss laced with despair and loss.

I can't stop the tears. I can't stop my hands from shaking. But I run to the florist and buy three dozen red roses, long-stemmed with thorns, the way you like them. On the way back, I brave the mall and buy a fresh bottle of your favorite perfume.

One day becomes two. One week turns three. No trace of flowers in the air. No new photos. I'm still alone with empty arms and a knot in my chest. I smoke cigarette after cigarette. Pace footprint divots in the carpet. Choke back tears as the hope leaks out, a little more with each passing day.

My boss was wrong about the wine. It doesn't help at all. Nothing does.

After two months, I slide the photographs into an envelope, tuck the flap over as best as I can, and pull a battered shoe box out from under the bed. Nine sets of photos. Ten envelopes, the last one sealed. The paper clearly reveals two small circular shapes. The saint on the medallion never offered assistance; the ring is only a circle of empty without your skin to bind it.

When I close my eyes, I recall every plane and curve of your face, before illness turned you pale and hollow, but I wonder, if not for the photographs, would I? Would time have turned my heart to scar instead of open wound?

I shove the box back under the bed, my mouth downturned. I should've known better. You've tried nine times in five years, and all the want in the world can't bring you back.

The next time my coworkers ask me to go to happy hour, I say yes. I say yes the second and third time, too. By the fifth time, I don't have to force a laugh at a joke or fake a smile when someone catches my eye. I feel a loosening in my chest, an ease in my breath.

I take the box of photographs and put them on the top shelf of my closet. I make sure all the doors and windows are locked before I go to bed. And, finally, I take off the silver ring. My eyes burn with tears, but I blink them away before they fall.

"Please let me go," you whispered through cracked lips. "Please."

"Never," I said, arranging the scratchy hospital blanket around your shoulders.

Your bare scalp was hidden under a yellow scarf, but nothing could hide the matchstick legs, the grey tinge of your skin, or the pain in your eyes that morphine couldn't touch. No amount of perfume could mask the shroud of illness and breaking hearts.

I held your hand and told you for the thousandth time about that night, our first date, after I dropped you off. How I turned and saw you standing with your hair full of moonlight and your lips full of smile. How I knew I would spend the rest of my forever with you.

"Please, baby, please."

And then only silence. I sat with your hand in mine until your skin began to cool, and I didn't cry until a nurse led me out of the room.

I wake on a cool morning in early autumn to find the photograph on the mat outside the front door. The lock of hair, the little smile, the pale roses. I stand with my hands in my pockets for a long time, but eventually I carry the photo back into the house.

I'll leave the windows open every night, weather be damned. I'll put flowers out every day. Because you were so close the last time, so very close, and that has to mean something.

I slip the ring back on my finger. It was a mistake to take it off in the first place. I won't make it again.

Please, baby, find your way back home to me. I'll wait for you no matter how long it takes. I promise I will. If you make it all the way this time, I'll say the goodbye I should've said in the hospital.

Maybe then I'll be able to let you go.

Immolation:
A Love Story

❧ ❦

Derek tells the woman the shoes are too small, but she insists on pushing her foot in and the flesh bubbles over the edge. When she teeters around the aisle, he winces. The stiletto heels are meant for a gazelle, not a cow. Her shiny, fat face splits into a smile.

"I'll take them," she says.

Derek wipes his hands on his pants and gives her the slick salesman's grin he's perfected countless times in the mirror. "Would you like to wear them out of the store?" Of course, she says yes.

The matchbook in his pocket is heavy, a dangerous weight to carry. He'd like to burn her up. After her skin blackened, the fat would go fast, sizzling away in a scummy pile of stinking yellow excess. He turns away so she can't see the light creeping up into his eyes.

After she wobbles out of the store, Derek goes into the back to wash the feel of her off his hands. The bell over the door chimes. Slipping on his pleasant, safe face, he heads back just in time to see her walk in, all stiletto heels and red lipstick. 38-26-36, he guesses, bought and paid for with her ex-husband's money and maintained with hours at the gym, sweating under the guidance of her personal trainer. The kind of woman who drinks dirty martinis with four olives, not three. A mannequin, ice-cold and perfect, but hot enough to burn the skin from his lips.

"I'm looking for a pair of black heels," she says. "Four inch stiletto heels."

Derek uncurls his voice from the back of his throat. "Size eight?"

Her full lips curve up at the corners. "Yes, how did you know?"

"It's my job."

She sits down and stretches out her long legs. The heat from her core pushes flames from her skin, flames only he can see. In the stockroom, he wipes sweat from his brow as he pulls out several boxes of shoes.

She shakes her head at the first pair, frowns at the second, but when he opens the third box (four inch heels, shiny patent leather, a tiny lace bow at the back), a quick laugh emerges from her throat like a butterfly escaping the chrysalis. "Those are perfect," she says.

Her toenails are painted the color of fresh blood. His hands shake as he slips the shoes on her feet, careful not to make contact with her skin. She's burning him up with her presence.

The muscles in her calves flex as she walks with graceful, practiced steps, leaving behind sex-heat, want-heat. Derek digs his fingernails into the soft flesh of his palms, tattooing his skin with half-moon bruises.

"What do you think?" she asks.

Too beautiful to burn, too gorgeous not to.

"You're right. They're perfect," he says. "Would you like to wear them now?"

"Oh, no, these are for a very special occasion. I don't want to ruin them."

After she sits back down, he removes the shoes, resisting the urge to touch. To feel. The matchbook falls from his pocket when he leans over to pick up the box, and they reach at the same time. Their fingertips touch, and a tiny spark of electricity jumps in the no-space between their skin. A strand of her hair falls forward, curving in a comma against the pale of her cheek. Her lips part; her fingers tremble.

Could it be?

He flips the matchbook over in his hand and puts it back in his pocket, watching her face the entire time. Her eyes are an ocean of lava filled with needwantmusthavenow. It explains everything.

They walk side by side to the register, not speaking. When he hands back her credit card, their fingers touch again; her heat pushes into his. He slips the matchbook into the bag with her shoes.

Will she understand?

Five minutes after she leaves, he calls the credit card company. His story is convincing, and they give him her address.

That night, unable to resist the heat within, he watches and waits. The second night, he lights one match after another, seeing her face in each tiny flame. On the third night, his perfection emerges from her house with her body encased in black, the new shoes shimmering like the carapace of an exotic beetle.

He follows her car at a safe distance, smiling when she reaches her destination, a new development where huge half-built homes silhouette the sky with their wooden skeletons. She gets out of the car and walks her heat-walk across the grass. A pregnant moon, haloed in red, lights the way. The moth-like flutter of his heart cannot resist the lure of her warmth.

The house (their house) is a shadow-maze of new wall smell. The glow from the moon reaches down through the unfinished roof, and her heels click on the floor with soft, gentle stiletto clicks. Another sound then, a quick little snick, and a smell he knows all too well—the sweet perfume of burning wood. The intoxicating scent of power.

When he finds her, her face holds no trace of surprise.

"I've been waiting for you," she says, holding up his gift, the matchbook, her voice whisper soft and honey sweet.

A snake-trail of fire winds its way around them, red-orange-yellow flames that flicker and hiss. Music, such sweet music, each note reflecting in the patent leather of her shoes.

"I knew tonight would be special." She smiles her red, red smile, takes his hand, and together they burn.

Part III

And Away

Melancholia
in Bloom

✌ ✍

*E*very family has a secret magic tucked away in a dusty attic or hidden
between the words of a handed-down story. This box is ours. It
doesn't look like much, but it's been in our family for a long time.
*After my mother's death, I found it in her attic with a notebook inside. Now I'll
leave the box for Rebecca. I hope she won't just think it an old woman's fancy.*

*My mother kept scraps of fabric. I was surprised to see neither a trace
of fading nor a moth hole. The tiny bits could have been snipped free from
their dresses yesterday. I will confess I didn't believe her words, not until I
touched one of the pieces. I won't tell Rebecca what I saw. I'll let her discover that herself.*

*Perhaps it's only a vanity. The mother not quite willing to let go of her child.
Who knows? It's almost silly, this keeping hush. I should just tell Rebecca in
person instead of writing it down, but would I have believed my mother?*

I'd like to think so.

I hate this place—the smell, the withered limbs hidden behind
each door, the traces of withered lives hanging in the air. No one
comes here to get well, only to wait.

My shoes tap on the tile floor; the sound hovers in the air
for a quick instant, then the walls tuck it away. I brought yellow
roses this time, and I hold them away from my body so the
stink won't linger on my clothes. My mother has never understood why I don't like them; I've never understood why she
does.

I take a deep breath before I enter her room and put on a smile
that should feel normal by now, but it doesn't. It feels like a lie.

When she sees me, her eyes narrow, her lips thin. The nurse acknowledges me with a nod and pats my mother's arm. Adjusts the sheets around her frail body.

"Helen, look, it's Rebecca, your daughter," she says a little too brightly.

My mother would hate this false cheer. I know she would.

"It's a beautiful day today, isn't it?" I say. To fill up the silence, to pretend.

"Well, I'll leave the two of you alone," the nurse says as she makes her exit, pulling the door shut behind her.

Images flicker across the screen of the television in the corner, but the volume is so low, even the commercials seem little more than a soft hum. I busy myself with arranging the flowers in a vase. My father always gave her yellow roses on her birthday. It isn't her birthday, but at this point, it doesn't matter.

The yellow petals should bring a touch of brightness to the room; instead, they bring a sharp sting of hurt deep inside my chest. I turn to see my mother watching me, her eyes wary. The expression turns her face into a stranger's. Another thing that should feel familiar by now, but even after six months, it doesn't.

"Sarah couldn't come today, Mom, but she sends her love."

In truth, I don't want Sarah to see her grandmother this way. I sit beside the bed and take her hand, her skin like tissue paper crumpled then pressed flat again. She pulls away. Makes a gravelly sound low in her throat.

I look down at my lap and think about the day Sarah was born. I remember the way my mother held her close, tears glittering in her eyes, as if it were yesterday instead of eight years ago. The way her voice caught when she sang a lullaby, the same lullaby she said she once sang to me. I push the memory away and babble about nothing until finally, I let the words fade away. What's the point? My mother isn't here anymore.

Something is…off. I jump at shadows. I can't remember if I locked the door. Last week, I went to put the laundry in and found towels sitting in the washing machine. From the smell of mildew, they'd been there for several days.

This morning, I couldn't find my keys. I spent an hour trying to find them, and when I did, they were hanging from the hook where I always put them. It was strange. I've never been the forgetful type. Maybe it will pass.

My father gave my mother roses for her birthday, their anniversary, for no reason at all. She would always pluck one petal from the roses. Only one. I asked her why once and she smiled, but she didn't answer. I'm sure I do silly things that make Sarah shake her head, too.

Every time I buy the roses, I hope they'll trigger something, some spark that will bring her back, even if only for a moment. Silly, I know.

There are gaps, spaces where names for things used to be. I'd convinced myself it was nothing more than old age, but today, after I went to the supermarket, I sat in the parking lot with my car running, trying to remember if I needed to turn right or left. I wasn't truly scared, but confused. I remembered what the house looked like. I remembered the street name, but I had no idea how to get there.

Luckily, I saw my neighbor, Emma (I remembered her bright yellow Volkswagen without a problem), and I followed her. None of the streets looked familiar, and by the time she turned onto my street, my hands hurt from holding the steering wheel so tight.

I lied. I was frightened. I know I should call the doctor, but that would make it real.

Even now, I replay the day before I found her over and over in my head. Was there something, some clue in her behavior? Her speech? Sarah was running around. Was it possible I missed a forgotten word, a dropped name, in the noise?

She made us lunch. She even cut Sarah's sandwich into triangular shapes—something that Sarah had only started requesting two weeks earlier. If she remembered something like that, how could a day, one single day, strip it all away?

The only thing odd was the way she hugged me before we left. A little tighter, a little longer than normal, and she looked as if she wanted to tell me something. Then Sarah tugged my hand; Mom patted my arm and told me to go. I felt her watching us walk to the car, and I swear she was watching as we drove away from the house. It's probably my imagination, though, embellishing the memory with a wish.

I was cleaning today, and I knocked the box aside. Nothing spilled, thank goodness, but one red petal was sitting on the edge, ready to fall. When I

touched it, I felt the tingle on, under, my skin, like I did when I touched my
mother's fabric scraps. And then it was as if something swooped in and filled
up all the spaces in my head.

It was extraordinary. I had no idea the box, the magic, could do this.
But I need to remember that these petals belong to Rebecca, not me.

She didn't answer the phone, which wasn't like her, so I went to her
house after I dropped Sarah off at school. I found her sitting dull-
eyed in her living room, still wearing her nightgown. She cried when
I talked to her, shrieked when I took her hands, screamed when the
paramedics arrived. But what else was I supposed to do?

I was so sure it was something small. Maybe a seizure or a fall
that clouded her thoughts. They gave her a sedative, and as I followed the ambulance to the hospital, I couldn't remember if I
told her I loved her the day before. I still can't remember, but I
have to believe that deep inside, she knows.

I told myself it was a fluke. My imagination. My hands were shaking when I
opened the box, but I had to try it again. I'm sure Rebecca would understand.
I know she would. I took one petal out, cupped it in my hand, and felt the
soft whisper of magic beneath my skin. A dance without music. A dream
without sleep. Like before, the empty spots inside me, inside my head, van-
ished; like before, it didn't last long enough.

Magic never does.

She babbled the first two months, but everything that came out
was a jumble of chaos. Once or twice, I thought I heard her say
my name, but no matter how many times I tried to talk to her, she
cringed away. I told her stories—the time we went to the beach
and I got stung by a jellyfish. How after my tears dried, I realized
that she, too, had been stung. The night of my junior prom and
how she drove me crazy asking for one more photograph. Just
one more. The day of my wedding when she gave me a lace-edged
handkerchief that once belonged to her great-grandmother, and
how she waved her hands around my eyes so my tears wouldn't
run down and ruin my makeup.

I kept waiting for her to wake up, to come back. I brought roses; she tore the petals from one of the blooms and held them tight
in her fists, muttering incoherencies all the while. When I took the

rest away, she screamed and pulled my hair. I didn't bring them again until her words vanished and the light in her eyes faded.

I used another petal. I felt terrible taking away another piece of something Rebecca should have, but she'll be here soon and I don't want her to see me that other way. She'll worry. She'll insist I call the doctor.
  I hope she'll forgive me. I hope she'll understand.

I drive to the facility like I do every week, but today I sit in the parking lot with the engine running. The building looms like an empty hotel with each window a glittering reminder that once upon a time there was joy and laughter. Little of that here, now.

  Once, we went on a camping trip to a cabin in the mountains and in the middle of the night, I climbed into my parents' bed because the noises terrified me. My mother told me the bugs and the forest animals were having a party, and if I listened very carefully, I would be able to hear them laughing. She didn't make me go back to my own bed, though. She simply scooted over so I had enough room. I was young, younger than Sarah is now.

  My fingers tighten around the steering wheel. My knuckles turn white. I can't do it. I can't face the stranger today. She doesn't know who I am anymore; she won't know I wasn't there.

  I hate this. I hate all of it. Tears well up in my eyes. Spill over my lashes. As I drive away, I promise myself I'll come next week. I just can't face her today.

My fingertips grow cold when the magic starts to fade. My thoughts twist and turn, and the words spiral out to nowhere. A ribbon I can't catch, no matter how hard I try.

One week turns into two. Then three. I go back on a rainy Sunday afternoon and get out of my car quickly, before I can change my mind. The nurse smiles, but I see the accusation in her eyes. I don't smile back.

Rebecca is coming over today. I sat with the box for an hour, afraid to use another petal, but too afraid not to. Is one more day with my daughter too much to want?
  In the end, I plucked one from the box and held it tight in my hand. My skin danced and I felt the missing words, the missing spaces, return. I felt like myself again. I felt alive.

What will happen when I forget the magic inside the roses? When I stumble around in my apartment, frightened by the sights and the sounds, like a drowning woman in a dark ocean of forgetting? When I forget that the box is my life pre-server? When I touch the roses, they say, "Helen, your name is Helen."

What will happen when I forget they're telling the truth?

When the doctor said she had Alzheimer's, all the air rushed from my lungs. I barked a laugh. Maybe I'd misheard. "When I saw her yesterday, she was fine."

I hid my hands so he couldn't see my fingers twist. The doctor said nothing, but I saw in his eyes that he thought I was lying.

"We spent all day together," I said. "All day. She was perfectly fine. And I saw her a week before that and she was fine then, too. I would have seen something if, if…" The words got caught in the tears I couldn't hold back. For several long minutes that felt like hours, I cried into my hands, feeling the weight of his gaze.

"In this stage, sometimes patients do exhibit moments of clarity. The disease affects everyone differently, and," he added kindly, "sometimes we see what we want to see."

But I know who I saw. My mother, not a stranger.

The box is half empty now. I should stop. I know I should. But I don't want to give Rebecca up yet. I don't want to give up myself yet. I hope she doesn't hate me for this.

I brought pink roses this time. My father gave them to her some-times. Not often, but enough. When I was a teenager, I finally real-ized the pink roses were apologies. After I put the flowers in the vase, I turn around. Her eyes are blank; her mouth slack.

I take a deep breath. "We have to sell your house, Mom. I'm so sorry, I didn't want to, but we can't afford not to, and I refuse to put you in one of those other places, especially since we don't know how long you'll be…here."

She says nothing. I know she doesn't understand what I'm saying, but I fight the urge to wither beneath her gaze. After a time, I kiss her forehead and smooth back her hair.

"I'll see you next week," I say.

I take her hand. She doesn't pull away, but I might as well be holding a mannequin.

I'm afraid. I'm so afraid. There's only one petal left and Rebecca and Sarah are coming over today. I should save it for her so she'll believe, so she'll save up little bits and pieces and tuck them away for Sarah, but I'm not ready to say goodbye.

Not today.

I stand in my mother's living room, staring at all the knick-knacks and what-nots. For a moment, I contemplate hiring several college students to come in and cart everything away, but then I see the tiny carved lion my father brought back from a business trip to Africa. Sarah loved to play with it when she was a toddler, and I was always afraid she'd break it, but my mother always brushed my concerns away with a small wave of her hand and a smile.

I start with her bedroom, boxing up things to donate and things to keep. In her jewelry box, I find a gaudy ring I bought for her at a school holiday sale and a bracelet of wooden beads Sarah made for her in kindergarten. I run my fingers over them and smile. I can't believe she kept all this stuff.

A wooden box I vaguely remember seeing when I was a child sits on her bedside table. When I open it, I smell a hint of roses and wave my hand in front of my face to disperse the scent. A diary, like something a teenage girl would keep, is inside the box. Funny, I never knew my mother kept a diary. I sit down on the edge of her bed and begin to read.

When Rebecca left, I tidied up. Made sure the laundry was folded and put away. Made sure the necessary papers in my desk were organized so they'll be easy for her to find. I can feel the memories starting to fade again. No matter how tight I hold on, they slip away.

I know I shouldn't complain. I've had a good life. I married a kind, loving man. I had a loving daughter. I regret I won't see my granddaughter grow to adulthood, but I'm grateful for the time I've had. Maybe I was greedy.

I hope I'm not too much of a burden. It hurts to forget, but sometimes it hurts even more to remember.

I put the diary down after I've read a few of the entries and scrub my face with my hands. I can't bear to read any more. Judging by the smell that clings to the wood, the box is where she kept all the petals she'd plucked over the years, but did she really think they were magicked into…something? It explains why she tried to tear apart the roses in the hospital.

How could I have been so blind? How could I have not seen the signs? It's obvious she knew something was wrong, and she was right about the doctor. I would have insisted she go. No, I would have *demanded*. If I had, maybe they could have slowed things down somehow. Maybe they could have done something. Why did she hide it from me? Did she think I'd love her any less? Then I think of the vacant eyes. The limp hand.

I cry until my throat aches. How I wish life was a children's story with magic and a happy ending instead of a memoir of illness and funeral plans.

With tears still in my eyes, I carry the box out to the pile of things to be donated. Maybe the disease made her think it was magic, but all it is now is a reminder of my failure. I tuck the diary in my purse. Maybe one day I'll read the rest, but I don't think so. I don't want to remember a woman rambling about nonsense. I'd rather remember her the way she was.

Rebecca,

I know I don't have long now. My fingertips are cold, and I can feel the pieces of me straining to break free. I hope you've found this diary. I hope you've read the words. I know it might seem crazy, but trust me. The box works. No matter what you choose to put in it, it will keep the memories tight until you take them out. I'm sorry I didn't save a petal for you to prove it, but please, you have to believe me.

Memories are the real magic, perhaps the only pure magic left in the world. Hold them tight as long as you can.

Please be kind to the old woman I will become. I have to believe that somewhere deep inside she remembers that you are her daughter and that she loves you.

Love,
Mom

Iron and Wood, Nail and Bone

❧ ❧

A dozen crosses—all wood, all occupied. Nails through wrists and feet. Low moans and whispers. Prayers. The smell of old coins cupped in a palm. The vinegar bite of perspiration. The salt tang of an ocean of tears.

The walls of the room are deep red; the floor black, sloping to a central drain. A woman steps around the crosses, checking wounds and temperatures and IVs.

Death is not the intention. Dying isn't the point.

Know this: no one will judge you here. No one will judge your need to be here.

You don't know if you're supposed to explain why you're here, but you feel the words pushing against your lips, straining to break free. If voiced, will they help? Hurt? Do they even matter?

The woman holding a gown in her hand shakes her head, and the words slip back down your throat. You wonder how she knew. You wonder what she sees in your eyes. You wonder why you're even here, how it all happened. You never thought you were the kind of person to end up in a place like this.

(Maybe that's a lie; maybe a place like this is exactly where you knew you'd end up.)

Your hands tremble when you take the gown, the fabric soft against your skin. It feels wrong; it should be coarse, a hair shirt worn for penance, not thin gauze shaped like a chiton on a Greek statue. This gown is meant for poetry, for beauty, not blood and nails. Something inside you twists. It's not too late.

(It was too late the moment you walked through the door.)

After you've changed, the woman nods toward a door. You swallow hard. Force your feet to move. The door makes barely a sound when it shuts behind you.

It's not what you expected.

(It's exactly what you expected.)

The crosses have been arranged in a circle. Only one of the twelve is empty. Waiting for you, waiting like a lover with rage for eyes and razors for teeth. You try not to look too closely at the others, but you can't help it. The nails, the blood, the sorrow. A dark perfume; an invocation in the air; a breathless song of suffering.

You want some sort of validation, some acknowledgment, but no one is paying you any attention, not even the man standing next to the empty cross.

(You can't bring yourself to call it yours yet.)

As you close the distance, your mouth turns dry, and your heart flutters bird wings beneath the cage of your ribs. You don't want to be here.

(You need to be here.)

The man's hands are strong but gentle as he lifts you up, arranges your feet on the tiny platform, and slips the IV needle into your vein with little effort, the bag hanging hidden behind the cross. There are no narcotics in the bag, only fluids to insure you won't go into shock.

When he lifts the hammer, his gaze finally meet yours. You have the choice to say no, to walk away. When you nod, his eyes hold no surprise, only a weary sort of sadness. Then he presses the first nail against your skin, brings the hammer down. You close your eyes when you hear metal strike metal, hear a thin scream that doesn't sound human. The pain is a shock that strips all thoughts from your mind. You didn't know it would be like this.

(You need it to be like this.)

You open your eyes, see blood flowing from the wound and clench your jaw, sure the red doesn't belong to you, sure this is some strange mistake, but you won't say stop. You close your eyes when you see the hammer lift again. It takes longer than you thought it would; it happens faster than you thought it would.

"Be well," the man says before he leaves the room.

In spite of the pain, you want to laugh. You can't imagine being well. You can't imagine anything but the agony in your wrists and feet.

But after a time, you lift your head. Gaze at the red walls, searching for a distraction or perhaps absolution. And then you see the suggestion of faces; look longer and the suggestion becomes something more, a tableau vivant.

A woman cringes in front of a man standing over her, his face contorted with rage, his fists moving one-two-three, and she doubles over, falls, and he kicks one-two-three as if it's some strange game of sadistic symmetry.

A man finds an empty liquor bottle on the counter and a woman passed out on the floor while a toddler with a soiled diaper sits beside her, crying, crying, crying.

A woman waits with a phone in her hand, pacing divots in a carpet while elsewhere, a man laughs with his wife, sneaking sidelong glances at his own phone when he thinks she isn't looking.

And when you see your own face, you close your eyes, unable to bear the sight or the shame. With your eyes closed, you can pretend it wasn't you. At least for a little while.

The ache pulses inside you, a feral child chewing you apart, ripping off tiny bits and pieces and swallowing them whole. You bow your head and weep silent tears that burn and burn and burn.

You don't want this pain.

(You need this pain.)

You don't want this pain.

(You crave this pain.)

You don't want this pain.

(You deserve this pain.)

When the session is done, your wounds are cleansed and bandaged, and you schedule your next appointment.

(Because of course you'll come back.)

The next time, you dare yourself to keep your eyes open, to watch the hammer, and for a moment, you think you're in a movie. This can't be you. This can't be your life. Then the nail slips in, piercing your skin, leaving you open-mouthed and gasping for a reason, a justification. You're the animal expecting a gentle touch instead of a kick from a cruel owner, a fool expecting things to change.

And you know you deserve all of it.

The hurt travels from wrists and feet, spreads all through your body, until it's the only thing you're aware of. This is okay.

(This is not okay.)

The images dance on the wall, blending one trauma into another, and tears come in a rush, hot and hard. You bite your lip to stifle the sound, convinced you'll never stop crying, never stop hurting, never be anything more than what you are at this moment.

When it's over, you take a dozen deep breaths, feeling your lungs expand and release, expand and release. Something so simple shouldn't be so hard.

The cross holds a sort of comfort now. A broken and twisted comfort, but comfort nonetheless. You can't remember anything *but* the cross, the rough wood against your back, the splinters in your skin. You've lost count how many times you've been here; you look forward to the first nail, the bite that says you're here of your own volition.

The pain washes over you—a baptism, a benediction.

You weep openly, loudly, not caring who hears. You know you're here because of the broken pieces of you, but there's a sort of safety in this. To glue your pieces back together takes a strength you know you don't have. It's easier to stay shattered. To suffer. To bleed.

The nails slide into your skin, the blood wells, runs, yet the pain is distant, indiscernible. You shift and splinters dig tiny hollows into your skin, but you feel nothing. You move again, tug your hands against the nails. Nothing.

It used to hurt. You know it did, but you can't remember quite how. You want to remember, to feel something, anything at all. Does this make you an emotional masochist, needing anguish to feel real, to feel of worth? Does this make you a ghost? Does this make you anything at all?

You try to make yourself cry, but tears will not come. You pray to a God you're not sure you believe in anymore, and you're not even sure what you're praying for. A miracle of hail and healing? A scourge of grasshoppers and plague?

You see the imagery on the walls, all the broken and the lost, but all you feel inside is cold. So cold, so numb, so nothing.

He brings the hammer, the nails, and your fingers twitch. Your eyes narrow. Haven't you bled enough? Haven't you paid enough?

He presses the point of the nail against your wrist, and you yank your arm away.

"No," you say, your voice thick and rusty.

You don't want to do this anymore.

(You don't need to do this anymore.)

You tip your head back and shout to the ceiling, a long, word-less shout as if your soul is raging against the world, raging against some machine of circumstance, against all the poor choices you were too blind to see. But now you see everything in stark de-tail—the black, the white, the grey. The sharp edges, the quick-sand centers, the pretty façades that hide their ugly far too well.

When the echo of your voice fades, the man puts the hammer aside. He smiles. Takes you down from the cross, presses a kiss against your forehead, places the nail in your hand and curls your fingers around it. You can't speak. It can't be that easy. All you said was no.

When the door shuts behind you, you take a deep breath. Tears shed the sorrow from your eyes. Your hands are shaking, but you hold tight to the nail. Something to hang the memories from or something upon which to impale them?

Your scars haven't healed, and they may never, not complete-ly, but you don't have to be ashamed because they'll serve as re-minders that you were stronger than you thought you were, that your spine may have bowed beneath the weight, but it didn't break. You're not sure what comes next, but your feet move for-ward, away, and you know everything will be okay eventually.

A dozen crosses—all wood, all empty. The IV bags hang like abandoned chrysalises. Those who were able to move on have; those who were not were carefully taken down, their wounds cleansed, their bodies wrapped in white, their names remembered or not.

There is always a cross here for you. Pray you never need it. Pray you never understand.

And All the World Says Hush

꙳ ꙳

S he walks down the street, high heels clicking on pavement. Long hair the color of fresh honey, a pink flower tucked behind one ear, and tanned legs peeking out from under a diaphanous skirt. She smiles here and there, and purchases coffee from a corner shop. People stop and stare. She pays them no attention.

Her eyes hold a million secrets and give up none. She could be a model or the girl next door. A princess or a harpy. Like hourglass sand, she slips by, her legs moving in wide strides.

"Beautiful," an old man whispers. "Like a girl from the forties."

"Hey, hey, hey," a construction worker calls out, sweat turning his shirt to dark circles.

She hears only the cicadas buzzing in the trees and the blood rushing through her veins. As she moves, she inhales the thoughts and whispers and turns them inside out. Each one leaves a stain beneath her skin, leaves her ready for dissection. Obsession. Bifurcation into lady and whore. Or madness and love. Her lips, dressed in gloss pink, lift into a smile, or perhaps a cleverly concealed scream.

She moves on. Streets become blocks; blocks become houses stacked up in neat rows with bay windows and wrought iron gates. Faces peer through the glass, eyes wide and watchful. She drinks in their secrets. All the little lies tucked into back corners and covered with dust. Houses become vacant lots. Broken fences. Shattered glass. Battered men and women in tattered coats, their dirty faces slack-jawed as they wait for time to pass. She takes in the sorrow. The emptiness.

"Spare some change?" one asks.

"Go away. Leave us alone," another mumbles, her mouth filled with the solemn absence of teeth.

The voices flicker away as she steps through a shadow and into a hidden door. Inside, all is quiet. All is still.

She retreats to a room at the top of a narrow staircase and begins to strip away her glamour. Her heels cease their clicking. Her skirt puddles on the floor. She wipes away a makeup mask of ivory, rose, and grey and drops the colors one by one into a porcelain sink.

What remains is egg-smooth, featureless. She could be an illusion or a shadow seen from the corner of an eye.

When the sun disappears, the girl climbs into a bed, and the world swallows her whole. The sheet flutters down and falls flat, without curve of hip or shoulder to change its shape.

Elsewhere, an old man dreams of tangled limbs and breathless sighs. A construction worker dreams of a girl he once knew, a girl he loved and let go. A homeless man hears the rustle of coins in a cup and wakes to find his cheeks damp with tears.

And cicadas sing beneath a moon the color of cottage cheese.

They Make of You
a Monster

↣ ↢

When the footsteps approach, Isabel scrambles to her feet. She staggers; spots of light dance in front of her eyes. Two days without food. Two days without water. She backs up until her spine presses against the stone wall. Tucks her hands behind her. She knows it won't make a difference.

She tells herself she won't scream.

The Healers, three women draped in robes of red, enter her cell. They don't say a word. She keeps silent when they grab her. Twists away from their grasp. Fights against them with all the strength she can summon.

It's not nearly enough.

Then they snap the first finger, the pinkie on her right hand. The pain is white. Blinding. Below the pain, a sensation of leaking. Emptying.

Her cries echo off the stone. From another cell, she hears shouting. One of the Healers laughs.

By the fifth finger, she doesn't have the strength to struggle anymore.

By the eighth, she can't even scream. Wavery moans slip from her lips. The greedy stone walls gobble them up and wait for more.

By the tenth, the world is grey, flickering in her vision like candleflame.

After the last snap fills the air, the Healers weave a spell to fuse her bones back together, to fill her up with something new.

When they let her go, she crawls to the corner of her cell, holds her ruined hands to her chest, and sobs into the filthy straw.

Midday, a guard shoves a bowl of porridge through the bars of her cell. Her stomach rumbles, but she makes no move for the food. If she does not eat, will they force it down her throat, or will they allow her to starve?

She knows the answer.

The porridge is bland, with neither milk nor honey to give it flavor, but she eats it all. She does not want to die.

Not yet.

At night, a guard walks the passageway between the cells. His feet tap a steady rhythm on the stone. He stops outside the bars of Isabel's cell, his face all sharp planes and angles, his clothing tainted with sorrow.

She pulls her knees up to her chin. What does he see? A young woman in a dirty dress or a monster in the making?

He runs his fingers along one of the metal bars, his skin safe behind leather gloves. All the guards wear them. For their protection.

"You knew it was forbidden," he says, his voice a blade.

She holds her tongue.

"You knew the risk, the penalty, yet you still did it. Does that make you brave or a fool?"

He walks away before she can take another breath. It is not her fault. What she is. She holds up her hands. What she *was*.

They've made her something else now.

They came for her two days after Ayleth fell. She doesn't know how they knew what she'd done. Perhaps someone was hiding nearby. Watching.

She pushes the thoughts away and thinks of Ayleth's dark hair, her green eyes, the way she laughed into the wind.

She feels it growing inside her, a darkness where before there was a spark of light. Their corruption.

If she had a knife, she would cut it out and leave it bleeding on the floor.

ҩ   ҩ

The guards bring in a girl whose face still holds tight to child-hood. Her fingertips leak thin grey trails of smoke. Her fire is spent. She does not fight against the guards' grips. She does not cry. She is already broken.

They put her in the cell across from Isabel's.

The girl screams when the Healers come. Isabel covers her ears. Had her own screams sounded so loud? So long? If her gift was fire, she would've set the straw in her own cell ablaze and burned herself alive.

Moonlight peeks between the bars of her cell's window, a window too high to reach, even if she stands on her toes. It does not matter, though. The only thing beyond her window is a rocky cliff facing the sea.

She closes her eyes, breathing in the stink of her own waste. The hopelessness of the stone walls. How many were in this cell before her? How many listened to the waves crashing against the rocks?

How long before they gave in?

She paces in her cell. The sun has turned the air thick and sticky, and the straw rustles with each step of her bare feet, scratching against her skin. They took away her shoes when they brought her here.

The guard in the passageway does not look in her direction. He does not look at any of them. He smells of roasted meat; her mouth waters.

The girl in the cell across from Isabel trembles, her teeth chatter, and ice crystals form on the straw beneath her. Is there even enough left of her inside to miss the warmth of her flames?

She is too young, far too young, to be so defiled.

"Let me see your hands, little fool," the night guard says.

She turns away so he cannot see them. Her heart races. Will he kill her? It would be a kindness.

Instead, he walks away.

She doesn't know why he wants to see. Nothing shows on the outside. She feels it inside, ugly and wrong.

They bring in an old woman. Her back is bent; her eyes, clouded with white. She cries for her children to save her, but no one will come except the Healers and the guards. Everyone knows that.

Isabel doesn't think it will take long for the old woman to give them what they want.

She dreams of drops of blood falling from the sky, of a field of knives littered with bones, and wakes drenched in sweat with a strange taste in her mouth of sour milk laced with ashes.

Her old magic, her *real* magic, tasted of ripe raspberries.

The guards take away a woman with long dark hair. She walks with her back straight and her mouth set in a thin line. Her eyes flash with defiance.

A door slams. After a time, muffled screams creep into the air and hang there for hours. When the guards bring the woman back, she smells of urine, vomit, the acrid tang of fear. She leaves a trail of blood on the stones.

The sight makes Isabel's stomach twist into knots.

The new king took the crown the year of her sixth summer. "You must never," her mother said, time and again. Even at six, Isabel understood why.

"Never, ever."

And she listened. Until Ayleth.

She thinks of Ayleth's broken body, the blood dripping from the corner of her mouth. What would happen if she touched her now? Would she be able to hold it in?

Finally, the guards come for her.

They bind her arms behind her back. Even with their gloves, they do not touch her hands. They lead her into a windowless room; the door shuts with a bang that vibrates in her teeth. The room smells of pain and sorrow. Of giving up. Giving in.

The man in the room smiles. A lie.

There is a table covered with a stained cloth, the fabric full of bumps and bulges. She does not want to see what the cloth is hiding.

"Will you serve your king?" the man asks.

She takes a deep breath. Doesn't answer.

She will not.

He does not remove the cloth from the table, he does not ask his question again, and the guards take her back to her cell.

Magic was not always forbidden.

When Isabel was a small child, there were no Healers, and only criminals were locked away. The old king was loved by the people, not feared. He loved balls, grandeur, music. The new king does not care for music, save that born of screams. Only those sworn to his service are allowed to wield magic; even then, they are only allowed a magic that has been perverted. Inverted. Fire to ice. Healing to—

No. She will not think of that now. She cannot.

Rumors say the king acts in cruelty because he secretly wishes he was born female. If so, he might've held magic. Instead, he has only his cock and the kingdom to grip.

But the why doesn't matter. Not here.

She dreams of Ayleth running toward her. Though Isabel runs as fast as she can to get away, to keep her safe, Ayleth won't stop.

She wakes just before Ayleth touches her hand.

They take the young girl out and do not bring her back. When the night wind blows cold through the window, Isabel thinks perhaps it is the girl, making ice for the king's wine.

The new magic inside her hungers. For what, she doesn't know.

She doesn't want to know.

The guards take her to the stone room again. The table is uncovered, revealing knives, hooks, spikes, and something shaped like a metal pear, something that screams malevolence. Anguish.

She feels the blood run from her face. Her fingers tremble.

"Will you serve your king?"

She swallows before answering. "No, I will not."

They laugh when they take her back. They know she will give in, eventually.

Or she will die.

She and Ayleth grew up in the same village, casting shy smiles at each other until finally, Ayleth kissed her behind the baker's shop.

Their love was not as forbidden as magic; people pretended not to see.

The day Isabel broke her promise of never, they were foraging for berries atop a wooded hill. In the distance, the spires of the castle gleamed in the sunlight. Ayleth paused with a handful of berries and whispered, "I would like to burn it down with the king inside."

"Do not say such a thing," Isabel said, casting a glance over her shoulder.

Ayleth shrugged. "There is no one to hear. Only us." She took a step forward. A twig snapped. Leaves crackled. Her mouth dropped open as her legs slipped out from under, and she tumbled down the side of the hill, her shouts punctuated with thuds and thumps all the way.

Isabel raced down as fast as she could without falling herself. At the bottom, she found Ayleth holding her belly, blood dripping from the corner of her mouth. Isabel tried to help her stand, but Ayleth shrieked and begged her to stop.

The village herbwoman would not be able to help. Not with this. In spite of Ayleth's protests, Isabel grasped her hands and let the magic out.

And the sensation... Her mouth flooded with the sweetness of berries, her fingertips tingled, and inside, it was as if butterflies were dancing soft beneath her skin. She felt it leave her body like a breeze through a window; as it flowed into her lover's, Ayleth's eyes brightened, her mouth formed a circle of surprise, then laughter bubbled up and out. They danced together like children, forgetting for a moment that, as proscribed by the king, the magic was wrong.

The guards carry out a body, laughing all the while. Isabel sees long dark hair. Pale limbs streaked with the telltale lines of blood poisoning. A face with blank eyes where defiance once lived.

The night guard watches her through the bars. She meets his stare, hiding her hands in the folds of her dress. She fears what they've done to her, fears who they've made her become, but she is not her hands. She is not their monster. She will not let it change her.

Yet she fears it already has.

❧   ❧

She stumbles as they push her into the room with the table. A skinny man with a ragged beard stands in the corner. His clothes are tattered. Shackles bind his bloodied ankles.

"Will you serve?" the man with the false smile asks.

"Never."

He nods at the guards. They hold her arms tight as they guide her toward the shackled man. The smell of his unwashed body makes her eyes sting.

"No, I will not do this. I will not."

But inside, the twisted magic says *yes*.

She struggles to break free. The guards shove her toward the man. She lifts her hands. A reflex. Not on purpose. When her skin touches his, when she realizes what she's done, it's too late.

Pain radiates through her belly like claws and fangs tearing free. Her fingers clench, digging into the man's flesh. She tries to hold the magic in, but it will not stay. She cannot make it bend to her will. It rips free, an animal in search of prey, and leaves the taste of rage in its wake. A vile brew filled with bitterness.

The man's eyes widen. His mouth opens. His face contorts in pain. His body spasms.

He falls.

For one quick moment, a feeling of power, of possibility, rushes through her. Then she shoves it deep down inside, and shame floods her. One of the guards nudges the man with his foot. He does not move. The liar smiles.

"Do you see what you are?" he says.

She closes her eyes. She doesn't want to see, doesn't want to know.

The night guard pauses in front of her cell again. Isabel wipes away her tears.

"They will take you from here when you agree. You will have meat, wine, clean clothes."

She shakes her head. She is not a monster. But she thinks of the man, the way it felt to take his life, and she shudders.

"Will you serve?"

"No," she whispers.

"You don't really want us to tear up your pretty flesh, do you?"

"I will not serve," she says between clenched teeth.

It is her turn to scream. To leave a trail of blood on the stones.

She dreams of the field of knives. Of Ayleth, her blood pouring from a wound Isabel can no longer heal, her arms outstretched. Isabel tells her no, but Ayleth doesn't listen. She grabs Isabel's hands and falls to the floor, her eyes open. Unseeing.

In her dream, Isabel laughs.

She wakes with a cry in her throat; her mangled body answers with a shriek of its own. She catches movement from the corner of her eye—the night guard, walking away.

Death came for her father in the shape of a lingering illness that caused his limbs to wither and his skin to turn grey. Her mother forbade her to help.

"I cannot lose you both," she said.

So Isabel held her magic in, no matter how hard it fluttered, yearning to help.

The twisted thing inside her now scrapes and pushes, burning to hurt.

The night guard taps the bars of her cell.

"What do you want?" she asks.

"Why do you fight?"

She doesn't answer. He would not understand.

"They're looking for your friend."

A whimper escapes before she can steal it back. Not Ayleth. Anything but that.

"Why do you care?" she whispers.

"The king's sister is next in line for the throne. She does not share her brother's penchant for cruelty. She would be a good queen, I think."

She looks up. He is staring at the window.

"The king is coming to the prison tomorrow. He is not happy with the progress of late." The guard steps close to the bars. Looks into her eyes. "He does not wear gloves," he says, his words so low that, save for the movement of his mouth, she might have imagined them.

The breath catches in her throat.

He gives her a small half-smile, the expression strange on such a harsh face. "You remind me of my sister."

As he walks away, she steps back with her hands held between her breasts. Why would he tell her such a thing?

How long until they find Ayleth? How long until they force Isabel to watch while they press the blades against Ayleth's skin? Her eyes burn with tears, and she covers her mouth to hold in the sound.

The waves crash upon the rocks. The wind blows in through the bars on the window. The cell fills with the smell of the sea.

She thinks of the girl who could make fire. The dark haired woman. The old woman crying for someone to save her. She thinks of all those living in fear, the ones they haven't found yet.

In the morning, she hears a strange coarse laugh. Heavy footsteps move down the hallway, and she steps close to the bars. Waits. The metal is cold beneath her fingers. The footsteps move closer.

Will they kill her once the king is dead?

She looks down at her hands. Her weapons. Not perverted. Perfected. The monster inside her extends its claws.

Let them try, she thinks. Let them try.

Paper Thin Roses
of Maybe

ở ớ

"Please don't be angry, Joshua," Maddie says. Her dark hair spills down over her shoulders; her blue eyes gleam grey in the candlelight.

"How can I not be angry with this?" He waves his hand toward the window, his shadow playdancing on the wall. Outside, all is somber, edged in sepia tones of a forgotten age, all moving closer, a little more each day.

"Please," she says. "Let it go."

"How can *you* not be angry?" he asks. "It won't be long now. It's coming faster now. It will be here, and we will—"

"Be immortalized forever," she says. "Someone will come along one day and say yes, I remember this. I remember them."

He laughs, the sound like broken glass ground in a fist. "There won't be anyone left."

"There is always someone left. Always."

He turns toward the window, giving her his back. He doesn't understand this new calm. She threw the phone across the room when it stopped working, hard enough to gouge the plaster wall. She cried for hours holding a photograph of her parents and screamed it wasn't fair.

He had no one to call. No one to mourn.

"Everything will be fine," she says.

He looks out over the city. Over what's left. A handful of streets, apartments, offices, department stores, the edge of a park. The trees on this side are heavy with green, the buildings all red brick and glass and shining metal faces, but on the other side, the flat side, they are brown and tan and cream, reminiscent of a snapshot from the early 1900s. Wind pushes past the window and blows the curtains into a fabric ripple. The wind travels past the buildings into the park, and the leaves shake and quiver. The other trees don't move, frozen in time with the rest of everything.

Above the sepia world, the sky is a shade of caramel; the clouds, buttermilk. In the real world, the sky is pale blue and threaded with wisps of white. As the clouds move across the sky and enter the other world, they stop and change color so quickly his eyes can't capture the transformation. When he glances at the place where movement ceases, a wave of dizziness, complete with sweaty palms and a racing heart, rushes over him.

He doesn't need to go to the windows that offer a view from the back of the building. It's there, too, creeping closer and closer every day.

"Nothing will be fine. Look at it." He jabs his finger toward the window. "Look at it."

She shakes her head. "I don't have to. I know what's there."

A tiny jingle-jingle drifts through the air, drawing his eyes down. A child is riding a tricycle in the street, pedaling in wide, disconsolate circles. A young mother stands off to one side with her arms wrapped around herself in a cocoon of make-believe solace.

Joshua closes the curtains and lights a cigarette, the smoke forming a halo around his head. Maddie's eyes narrow in disapproval. It doesn't matter, he almost says, but he holds his words inside. The little bell rings out again and disappears without an echo.

Maddie might not be afraid anymore, but he's afraid enough for the both of them.

"Come to bed," Maddie whispers.

He doesn't want to sleep (What if it comes during the night, freezing them in place in their bed?), but he slips beneath the blankets and curls his fingers around hers.

Once her breathing turns soft and even, Joshua climbs out of bed and leaves the apartment, locking the door behind him out of habit, not need. The streets are deserted, the silence absolute, and the pavement swallows up the sound of his passage.

He steps to the edge of the real city and gazes across the street, a once busy street that held shoppers, cars, taxis, a choking miasma of need and want and must have now. The air smells of apples turned sour and old perfume, but underneath, it holds the musty scent of cardboard boxes filled to bursting with old paper and ancient memories. He shivers, although the air isn't cold.

The sidewalk and most of the street is still real, still concrete and asphalt. He steps off the curb, takes two steps closer to the buildings, and stops in front of what used to be an office. Turning his body to the side, he stares down the street, at the line where real meets unreal. The buildings, depleted of their natural colors, are all one-dimensional and flat.

From the corner of his eye, he sees a woman dressed in a long black coat and white gloves, with a tiny hat balanced on the back of her head. She nods in his direction and continues walking. Joshua follows her, keeping a safe distance from the other world, until she comes to a stop, twenty feet down the street. "My children came here," she says. "They wanted to see. That's my daughter." She points to a woman with short hair and earrings dangling to her shoulder. "My baby girl."

"No, don't touch her," he cries, but he's too late, her hand is already reaching. The sepia pulls her in, expanding all the while to fit her into the tableau. In an eye blink, her coat turns mahogany and her skin a shade of parchment; her face wears sorrow mixed with expectation. Joshua backs away. The street has turned half grey, half walnut brown.

He runs all the way back, back to the apartment, back to Maddie, safe and real and warm in their bed.

They sit in the kitchen with the curtains shut and drink lukewarm tea and eat peanut butter and jelly sandwiches. After, he pretends to read while Maddie rummages around in their spare bedroom. When something crashes to the floor, he turns the book over on the table and finds her sitting on the floor surrounded by a tangle of forgotten things on her lap, an old lamp on its side behind her.

"What are you doing?"

She glances up, bright eyed, and smiles. "Remember the rose you made for me? On our first date?"

"The one I made from the napkin?"

"Yes." She holds up a battered and stained scrap of paper that resembles a squashed pumpkin with a long stem, not a rose. "I want to have it with me when it happens."

He sits on the floor and cups his hands around hers, the misshapen flower in the center of their grip. The night he gave it to her, he knew he wanted to spend his forever by her side. But not like this. Never like this.

"Maddie?"

"What?"

He tries to find the words, but a lump sits in his throat instead. When he finally chokes it down, he shakes his head, afraid he'll say everything wrong.

He goes outside again the next night and stands in the quiet. A clock above one of the building doors stands frozen at 11:15. He walks down to the woman in the dark coat. Her watch shows 2:23.

Time stopped, and the world stopped with it, he thinks.

He looks down at his own watch; the second hand ticks away the time. His time hasn't stopped yet, but it's close. When he leaves, his cheeks are wet with tears, tears he doesn't remember crying.

Two nights later, he returns and sits on the curb with his elbows on his knees and his chin in his hands. A wave of anger coils up from the inside, all scarlet and laced with thorns.

When Maddie sits next to him, his shout of surprise fills the air for one quick moment before it vanishes away. She slips her hand in his. "You shouldn't be afraid. Maybe there's life inside," she whispers. "And maybe we're just seeing the echoes."

"There aren't any echoes."

"Not on this side, no, but who knows what's on the other side."

"Maddie, there's nothing. Can't you see that?"

"If you're so afraid of it, why do you come here every night?"

He sits up straight. She smiles.

"I'm keeping an eye on it, that's all," he finally says.

"But why? It will come for us soon enough." She squeezes his hand. "Then we'll know."

He grabs her shoulders and gives her a shake. "What's happened to you? How can you be so damn calm?"

She takes his hands away one by one and presses a kiss to each palm in turn, her mouth warm against his skin. "I can't," she says in a small, quiet voice.

He bites back a sound halfway between a groan and a laugh. "What do you mean, you can't?"

"I know you don't understand, but I can't be angry. I can't be afraid anymore." Her voice breaks; she takes a deep breath. "I know it won't do any good, and if I start crying, I don't think I'll be able to stop. I pray every night that this is all a mistake, that everything will be fine in the morning." She squeezes her eyes shut and shakes her head. "It hurts too much to be afraid. It's better this way. Trust me."

"Oh, God, Maddie." He pulls her close.

She trembles in his arms, then pushes him gently away. "Let's go home."

"I'm scared, I'm so scared—"

She puts a finger to his lips. "Shhhh."

They make love long into the night and fall asleep with their legs entwined.

He wakes alone. He knows as soon as his eyes open; the weight of the apartment has changed, lifted, the trapped exhalation belonging only to one, not two.

No, oh, no. Please let me be wrong. She wouldn't leave me. Not like this. Not now.

She left a note, her handwriting spidery and thin, on a small scrap of paper lying in the center of the kitchen table, one edge held in place with the salt shaker, a silly ceramic pig they'd found at a yard sale.

Joshua,

I'm sorry. I couldn't wait any longer, and I knew if I told you, you'd try to stop me. I believe that when it's all over, we will be together again. Instead of saying goodbye, I will say until then. I love you.

Always and ever,

Maddie

He crumbles the note into a ball and throws it against the wall. Bites back a shriek. No, maybe he isn't too late. He flees from the apartment, not bothering to lock the door, and runs along the edge of the world where flat meets real, calling out her name, knowing she can't hear, but calling anyway. Tears pour down his cheeks, and the hurt turns every heartbeat to pain. He can't believe she's gone. He refuses to believe she's left him like this.

Then he skids to a halt. There. His Maddie. Standing with a small smile on her face and the paper rose held in one hand. Her other hand is extended, palm up, beckoning him closer. He steps as close as he dares.

"Why did you leave me? Oh, Maddie, why didn't you wait?"

He thinks about the paper flower, the way she'd tipped her head back and laughed when he'd presented it, feeling foolish, but right. The way her fingers curved around his own.

And the tears won't stop; he can't make them stop. He cries until his throat aches, until his eyes are swollen and the world is a blur.

I would've gone with you, if you'd asked me to. If only you'd asked. It isn't better this way. Not for me.

When he wakes the next morning, the buildings across the street are captured in russet and amber. He steps outside. The sidewalk in front of his building and most of the street is still safe. Still the color of real. Not the color of past.

He can no longer see Maddie, but he knows she is there.

Somewhere.

He hopes she isn't afraid. He hopes she isn't in pain.

A loud rumble of thunder wakes him from a deep sleep. Fat drops of grey are falling from the sliver of sky, dark clouds roiling in the small space.

He sits at the kitchen table with his head in his hands, listening to the storm cry its rage. After a time, he takes a napkin, folding it by memory, his hands sure and careful. When he finishes the first rose, he makes another and then another, until a dozen paper roses lay on the table. He leaves them there and fumbles his way back to bed, pulling the covers over his head to keep out the sound of the storm.

I'll see you tomorrow, Maddie. Tomorrow. Even if you don't know I'm there.

In the morning, rain still falls, but of a gentler sort, and mud spatters the street. Joshua drinks the last of the tea. It tastes like tears on his tongue.

He gathers the roses and ties them together with a purple ribbon, Maddie's favorite color. The soft coconut smell of her hair lingers in the apartment. He breathes it in, willing it to memory. Holding the roses against his chest, he traces his fingers over their wedding photograph and says goodbye to all the things they bought together.

Then he hears a shout, not of dismay, but wonder. With heavy steps, he walks to the window.

The rain has washed everything clean, and the mud isn't mud at all, but a mix of umber and sienna. All the colors have been stripped away, leaving behind a stark landscape of black, white, and grey.

He holds his breath as a woman approaches one of the black and white buildings and disappears around the side. He sinks to his knees when she returns. "You have to see this," she cries out, her voice rising up over the buildings. "Everyone, please, please, come and see!"

Several people emerge from buildings on the real side of the world, people he vaguely remembers from the time before, people he passed on the sidewalk or almost bumped into at the corner coffee shop. They all follow the woman, their voices trailing behind in syllabic streamers of anticipation.

Joshua races from the apartment and staggers across the street. All around him stands a forest of paper dolls and thin scraps of buildings, the fronts and backs pressed up against each other, the interiors locked away, tucked inside like flowers pressed between pages of a book.

He runs again until he finds her, motionless and still.

Ignoring the voices of those running in circles around him, shouting out 'whys' and 'hows' and 'what nows' (he doesn't care about any of their questions. He doesn't need reasons.), he touches Maddie's face. Her skin, the texture of good paper, warms beneath his palm. He clenches a fist to his chest. His heart hurts in a place he didn't know existed.

"I wish," he says, his voice thick. "I wish you'd held on just a little longer."

He swallows his sorrow. He will not leave her in the street. He can't. She belongs at home, with him, not here, and with gentle arms, he lifts her up. The weight is wrong, all wrong, but it will be better soon. He knows it will.

Careful not to bump her on the door or the walls, he carries her into their apartment, puts her in their bed, and tucks the covers around her shoulders, ignoring the way the sheet clings to flat lines and angles instead of curves. He sets the paper roses on the nightstand so she'll see them

if

when she wakes and sits on the floor beside the bed.

"Everything will be okay," he whispers. "I know it will."

As the sun moves across the room, his back aches and his stomach growls, but he's afraid she'll fade away into nothing if he moves. If he were a painter, maybe he'd know how to bring her colors back, but all he can do is hold still and hope.

When the room turns to shadow, he climbs into bed. Imagines he can hear a tiny, tiny breath forming deep in her lungs, waiting to emerge, waiting to push her back to real.

"Please come back, Maddie. Please come back to me. You're all I have."

He falls asleep with tears in his eyes, one hand curled under his cheek and the other holding her hand, dreaming of paper cuts and maybes and time.

Grey in the Gauge
of His Storm

೭ ❧

Pattern:

Every lining has a cloud, be it a worn spot, a mended seam, or an unraveled thread. They are neither perfect nor impenetrable, no matter how much we wish it so. People will tell you that damage makes the fabric stronger.

It depends on the damage.

Ease:

After the storm has passed, I look down at my arm, just above the elbow. The new tear in the lacework of my lining is small. I pull myself up from the floor and sit on the sofa, breathing hard. I feel as if I'm made of dandelion fluff, as if one puff will blow me into a million pieces, but this feeling, this small weakness, will pass.

I hear a cabinet open and close and wipe the last trace of tears from my eyes. Alan comes back holding a needle in his hand, but he doesn't meet my gaze, doesn't say a word, as he plucks a strand from his own lining without flinching, threads the needle, and stretches out my arm.

I turn my head away. The first stitch is always the worst, but this pain is different. This pain links us together even more. I stare at the wall, at a photograph of the two of us taken a few weeks after we met. Our hands are clasped, our shoulders touching, and I can see a hint of the tempest hidden in his eyes, but it isn't his fault. I must have said or done something.

I know better now. Tonight was a mistake. A stupid mistake.

He finishes, puts the needle aside, and strokes his fingers over the new repair. He's skilled. The stitches are barely visible; it will be easy to hide. And it doesn't hurt much.

Not this time.

His hand moves up; he traces my lower lip, then he cups my jaw. "I love you," he says, his voice hoarse.

"I love you, too."

He pulls me to him, hard against his chest. His lips crush mine. Maybe tonight we'll love everything away and the needle and thread will be a thing of the past.

His lining is burlap. Rough and strong. I trace it with my fingers when he sleeps. There are repairs here and there, but I don't know if he fixed them himself or if someone else's hand wielded the needle.

I asked him once. I won't ever do it again.

Give:

At work, I answer the phone, make client appointments, and deliver messages, but I watch the clock. I can't help it. The hours seem to drag, even when the office is busy.

At the end of the day, I rush home into Alan's arms; when he kisses me, I feel as if time has stopped. For us. For love.

I am lucky, so lucky.

Renee is sitting in the back of the coffee shop, her mouth turned down, checking her watch.

"I thought you were going to stand me up like the last time," she says.

I feel my cheeks warm. I'd forgotten about that. Alan and I had been talking, and I'd lost track of the time.

"I'm sorry."

"It's not a big deal. You're here now."

As always, her lining is shimmery. Perfect. It matches the light in her eyes. When we first met in high school, she held mine up to the light, didn't laugh at the worn edges, the threadbare center. She didn't ask how, but I told her anyway. We've always told each other everything.

"I feel like I haven't seen you in ages," she says.

"I know, I'm sorry. We've been busy."

She gives a small nod. She talks about her job. I tell her about the restaurant where Alan and I went last weekend. She raves about a book she recently read. I mention a new movie Alan and I want to see. We both order second cups of coffee. I scratch my arm, lifting my sleeve, and her eyes follow the motion. Her brow creases.

"What happened?"

I pull my arm back and manage a smile. "It's nothing. I'm clumsy, you know that."

"You've never been clumsy before."

She stares at me for so long, I feel like I'm withering. Then she looks away, and a strange hush hangs over the table. Eventually we fill it, but our voices hold a strange weight. Maybe we just don't have that much in common anymore.

Tack:

We call in sick and spend all day in bed. He makes breakfast. I make lunch. We watch movies and, in between, make love.

"I love you," he whispers in my ear. "I've loved you since the first minute I saw you. I knew you were the one. You are everything to me. I don't know what I'd do if I lost you."

"You'll never lose me," I say.

"Promise me. Promise you'll never leave me."

"I promise."

And I mean it. He is my everything, too. We make love again. My thighs ache; my heart aches even more. This is real. This is love. It's supposed to hurt.

Yoke:

I know I've said the wrong thing the second the words are past my lips. The apologies spill out like buttons from an overturned jar, but it's too late.

His mouth sets in a thin line, and his eyes go flinty dark. The storm rushes in. Pulls the breath from my lungs. Wind scours my cheeks; the crackle of electricity dances in the air. I want to run, but there's no way to escape, and if I try, it will only make things worse.

The first rip comes fast and hard, so quick it takes a moment for the pain to catch up. And again, the fabric splits with an ugly sound. I fall to my knees and pray this storm will have a quick end. I smell a sharp tang of metal and salt.

"Why do you make me do this?" he says over and over.

But we both know why. If my lining were made of denim, not lace, this wouldn't happen. Maybe if I'm torn apart and stitched back together enough, I'll be strong enough to make him happy all the time. I know he doesn't want to hurt me, not really. He wants me to be strong.

After the shriek of the wind dies down, he goes to fetch the needle. His hands are gentle, and when we kiss, I taste a ray of sunlight on his lips.

Maybe one day I'll be his sun.

"I love you," he says.

I know he does. I have three new sets of stitches as proof.

In the dark, I run my hands across my lining. Trace one fingertip along the new stitches. A part of him, now a part of me. I wonder if there are other women with threads of him still inside them, but I push away the thought before it can take hold.

It doesn't matter anyway. I am his everything.

"You shouldn't have to work so hard," he says one night when I come home late from the office. "We don't need the money anyway. I make enough for both of us."

My boss doesn't say anything when I tell her I'm leaving, but her eyes show disapproval. Or maybe it's just jealousy because she doesn't have anyone to take care of her.

Binding:

"You don't need anyone but me," he says.

"I love you," he says.

"Promise me," he says.

"I'm sorry," he doesn't say, but the needle and thread says it for him.

He takes me shopping.

He picks: a red dress, a black dress, a nightgown trimmed with pink ribbons.

I pick:

Renee calls. I reach for the phone, but he kisses me until I forget about everything and everyone else.

I cook his favorite foods. Pour his favorite wine. Breathe him in. Trace the stitches in the darkness. His. Mine. His. Mine.

Renee calls again. I don't answer.

"I don't need anyone but you," I say.

"I love you," I say.

"I promise," I say.

"I'm sorry," I say. "I'm sorry, I'm sorry, I'm sorry."

Facing:

He presents the ring one night after love. I hesitate a moment too long, but I don't mean to. The word *yes* gets caught in my throat, all tangled up in the want and the need and the thought of forever.

The storm blows in and out again, leaving behind a neat line of stitches below my right eye. The first I won't be able to hide. But it's okay because now everyone can see that I belong to him.

I sneak out to surprise him with coffee and bagels, and as I walk in the café, Renee is walking out. She stops. Pulls me aside. Touches my face.

"It's nothing," I say. "I bumped into—"

"Stop this," she says.

"What are you talking about?"

I step away because I need to get back before he wakes up. I should've left a note.

"What did he do?"

"Nothing, he did nothing. It was an accident."

She shakes her head. "What is wrong with you?"

"Nothing is wrong."

I need to hurry. I wish she'd shut up. When I take another step, she grabs my arm. Sees the ring.

"I don't know why you stay with him, but this isn't love. This is something perverse and broken. You are better than this."

I wrench my arm from her grasp. She doesn't know anything. She doesn't know the shape his mouth makes when he says my name, the spark in his eyes, the way I feel his touch on my skin for days, the way his stitches are making me whole. Of course it's love. If she were truly my friend, she'd be happy for me.

And she isn't right.

(Is she?)

I'm not broken.

Overcast:

"For always?" I ask.

"Of course."

I touch the ring to my lower lip. Gently, so as not to tug on the stitches there.

When he comes home from work, I see the gathering clouds. I keep my voice low. Tiptoe through the room. I don't ask him what's wrong. He'll tell me if he wants to, and if he doesn't, it isn't anything I need to know.

After we eat, I put on the beribboned nightgown, tug my hair from its ponytail, and give him the smile he likes best.

The clouds swirl anew. For the first time, I scream. He covers my mouth so no one will hear. One, two, three tears, and I feel the rips deeper and wider than ever before. He plucks threads from himself with a grimace, slides the needle in. He doesn't speak. Doesn't kiss me when he finishes, just tosses the needle aside and glares at me with empty eyes. No storm. No sun. Nothing.

The stitches are crooked, and I find a piece of lace on the floor. I hold it in my hand. This is the first time he's torn a piece free. I replay the night, trying to figure out what I did wrong.

When he falls asleep, I reach out my hand. The burlap is so rough, my lace catches. This pain is new. Different. But I don't make a sound. I know better.

"For always?" I ask.

"Finish your coffee," he says.

Tension:

I sense, not see, the clouds almost every day. His words hold the echo of thunder, the weight of a tsunami. The house fills with a hush. It hurts, this waiting.

I find strands of burlap on the counter. Entwined in the carpet. Stuck to the shower curtain. I collect them all and wish I could thread them back in while he sleeps but I'm afraid to try. I twist them together and tie them around my wrist instead.

I find bits of lace, but I throw them away.

He reaches for me in the night. I taste the heat of ozone on his lips. He pushes my face in the pillow, and we pretend to make love.

In the morning, there's a new tear in my lining. He sees the rip, I know he does, but he doesn't pull a strand of himself free. He doesn't get the needle. I don't know how to fix it, so I cover it with a scarf.

I remember our first date—wine and roses. A perfect cliché. After dinner, he walked me to my door, brushed my hair back from my face, and kissed me. He left so quickly, I barely heard his footfalls on the pavement.

He brought me a single rose on our second date. And on our third and our fourth. I don't remember how we went from there to here. I don't remember who I was before I met him.

(Would she recognize me?)

I call Renee, but when she answers, I hang up. She calls back, but I pretend not to hear the phone ring.

When the storm finally comes, there's no warning. There are no words. He pushes me to the floor and rips and rips and rips. I can't cry or scream, the pain is too big. I'm drowning in the waves and every time I come up for air, the wind pushes me back down.

I beg him to stop, to let me go. I hate the sound of my voice, the taste of my tears. And I go under again.

When the water recedes, my head is in his lap. He touches my cheek, my lip, brushes my hair back from my forehead.

"I'm sorry," he says.

But it's too late. I see pieces of lace caught between his teeth and under his nails. I pull free and try to crawl away, but he won't let me go.

He brings out the needle.

"No," I say. "No."

"Shhh," he says and plucks a strand free from his arm.

I stare at the wall as the needle slides in. It doesn't even hurt anymore.

I didn't know it would be like this.

But I love him

(Don't I?)

Hem:

He kisses me on the forehead before he goes to work. I curl up in the middle of the bed and trace my fingers over the stitches. I can't even see where he ends and I begin.

I pluck one of his strands free, and it leaves an ugly mark behind, all twisted and uneven. Maybe love always leaves scars. I reach for the needle, but my hands are shaking. I don't know how to fix this. I don't know how to fix *me*. Inside, I am cold, so cold, as if a blizzard blew in when I wasn't looking.

I pull another strand free. Then another. And another. Snowmelt blurs my vision, but my fingers don't stop. His strands aren't strong, they're sharp, cutting the soft pads of my fingers. The pain is bright. Hard. My mouth works, but not a sound emerges.

He would be proud of that.

The bed is littered with a hundred pieces of him and a hundred pieces of me that broke off in the process. My lining is full of holes, like a dress left too long in an attic trunk.

I climb out of bed. Arrange all the loose threads in the shape of a woman. She has no voice, no opinions, no needs. I slide the ring from my finger and slip it on hers. Maybe he won't even notice the change.

I wipe the tears away, but they won't stop, and my heart is a tangled knot. I struggle to catch my breath. Stumble as I try to walk. I think of calling Renee, but I'm afraid of what she might say. I'm afraid she might want to help, and I don't want her to see who, what, I've become.

Threads are still unraveling, falling to the floor in a trail of broken. He can have those, too. I leave the front door open behind me because if I touch it again, I might change my mind, and I know I can't. His threads were never meant to hold me together.

The clouds outside are grey, like my heart. I turn my face up to the sky, and rain mixes with my tears. I make it to the end of the street, turn right, and keep walking. More threads drift free. Am I a patchwork doll leaking from the seams or a snake shedding the old to reveal a new?

I don't know how far I'll get before my lining gives way completely. I don't know if I'm strong enough to face a sun. I don't know if there's anything left of me at all.

Like Origami
in Water

❧ ❧

Johnny is angry again. I hate this part, but I won't try to stop him. I would feel the same way, too.

"It's not fair," he yells, spit flying out of the corners of his mouth. "And it's not right. Why can't they figure out what this is? Why can't they fix it?"

Music blares from the speakers. The walls are paper-thin, but our neighbors aren't home, and Johnny shouts over the lyrics, demanding to be heard. He paces back and forth in our tiny apartment with its drafty windows, his walk an awkward, lurching stumble. He only has one toe left, the baby toe on his left foot. And in the space where his other toes used to be?

Nothing. Nothing at all.

"Eventually you won't even remember what I looked like," he says and sinks to the floor, holding his hands around his head.

I shut off the music and sit next to him, breathing in his scent, a soft, musky smell with something new hidden underneath, a smell like charred wood in a long dead fire. "That's not true."

"I'm only twenty-six years old. It's not fair." He holds out his arms. The inside of his elbows are marked with swirls of purple and yellow. "I'm not going back to the doctors anymore. What's the point? They don't have any answers. They'll just stick me in a corner room and stare at me like a circus freak."

I take a sheet of paper, the surface slick beneath my fingers, and fold it until a dragon appears. I learned how to fold paper from my mother, as she learned from hers. She told me her mother learned from Akira Yoshizawa, the great master of paper folding, when our family still lived in Japan. *Washi*, the traditional paper, is the best to use, but I make do with what I find in craft stores, even though it tears easily if I'm not careful. My mother says the best origami holds something inside—love or anger or hurt. Something to make it real.

I set the dragon on the floor next to my feet. Johnny saves them all, even the ones that turn out wrong. He lines them up on the windowsills and calls them his gargoyles. They're not watching out, but watching in. Watching him.

"I'm glad my parents are dead," he says. "So they don't have to see this." He grabs my hand and gives it a tight squeeze. "Will you stay with me all the way to the end?"

"I'm not going anywhere. I promise."

He leans over, rests his head on my shoulder. Tears burn in my eyes, but I hold them in. Johnny hates to see me cry.

A week later, his feet are gone.

After his legs vanish from the knees down, I make a red army of paper swans and set them on top of the refrigerator. He's sitting at the table, ripping paper into tiny shreds, and from where I stand, I can't see the missing parts and can almost pretend everything is fine.

I don't watch when he crawls to the bedroom, but the sound echoes back.

His knees disappear next.

"It hurts when they go," he whispers. "And even when the pieces are gone, I still feel them. I know they're gone, but I still feel them there."

Johnny's reading in bed when his fingers go. One minute he's holding the book; the next, it tumbles down onto the blanket, landing with a tiny thump. He gives a little grunt, and his mouth twists down. I know what I'll see, but I look anyway. His fingers are pale and vapory, narrow ghosts fading fast, and then they're gone, leaving behind a little more of that old wood smell and a little less of his.

"It was a stupid book anyway," he mutters.

I scoot over, not touching close, but close enough. He turns to me and presses his lips against mine, offering up what warmth he has left. He hasn't kissed me since he lost his feet.

In his kiss, I taste oranges and despair.

"Turn on the music," he says. "Please."

I do.

"Louder."

I turn it up until he nods. He shouts until the neighbors pound on the walls.

I turn the music down and make a bird, another dragon, and something that's supposed to be an elephant. A baby's wail creeps in through the plaster followed by the muted tones of an argument.

"Can you put that one on the nightstand?" he asks, his voice scratchy and dry, nodding toward the not-elephant. "That's my new favorite."

"But it doesn't look like anything."

He smiles, the first smile I've seen in weeks. "It does to me."

I put it next to the alarm clock.

The rest of his hands are gone. His wrists, too.

"Please don't forget about me," he whispers.

I wonder if there's another room somewhere, with someone like me, waiting, and another, like Johnny, going away.

I hold in my tears and pour my sorrow into a paper crane the color of a summer sky.

A week later, his arms vanish. He doesn't shout. He doesn't say a word. Instead, the silence hovers, a sharpened guillotine waiting to strike.

I make another elephant; this one turns out perfect. I unfold it, rip up the paper, and throw the pieces away before Johnny can see.

When there's nothing below his waist but air heavy with the scent of char, I sit in bed and he rests his head on my lap. I play with his hair and run my fingertips across his eyebrows. There's a knot inside my chest; with every passing moment, it twists a little more.

"I'm afraid," he whispers. "There won't be anything left to bury or burn. It'll be like I was never here. Say you'll remember me. Swear it."

"I won't ever forget you. I promise I won't."

"Can I have the elephant?"

I set it on his chest.

After Johnny falls asleep, I touch the empty space where the rest of his body should be. The knot inside me coils tighter. I stay awake for hours turning paper into shapes while the not-elephant moves up and down as he breathes.

"Zou-san, zou-san," I sing, keeping my voice feather soft. The words are part of a song my mother sang to me when my fingers were still too chubby to make paper animals.

But I can't remember the rest, no matter how hard I try.

When the end comes, it happens fast. I sit by his side, talking about nothing until a lump in my throat steals my voice away. I kiss his forehead, and he closes his eyes against the pain. The air shimmers like crushed pearls caught in moonlight.

"I love you, Johnny," I say, but he's already gone.

His voice whispers from the weightless spot beside me. "It doesn't hurt anymore."

Then that, too, disappears.

And all the paper animals, the stupid folded pieces of paper that mean nothing, nothing, watch from the windowsills.

With heavy steps, I go from room to room, stuffing them by the handful into a bag. Even through the plastic, I feel the weight of their gaze, straining to break free.

But I know how to make them stop.

I carry the bag down to the bridge where Johnny and I shared our first kiss, the best kiss. The river underneath, brownish-green in the fading light, rushes by; the muddy stink crawls inside my mouth and lingers in the back of my throat.

As the sun sets, I throw the paper animals into the water one by one. They bob on the surface, turning end over end, bright specks of color in the fading light, until the water swallows them whole. The blue crane, with its secret heart of sorrow, is the last one to drop out of sight.

I drop the bag, and the not-elephant tumbles out onto the ground. The air rushes out of my lungs; everything turns to a blur.

I cover my eyes to hold in the tears, but they won't stay inside. I can't make them stay.

The not-elephant still holds a trace of Johnny's smell, his real scent, not the stink of his illness. I cradle it to my chest, rocking back and forth while all the hurt he left behind spills out.

There isn't enough paper in the world to make it go away.

About the Author

Damien Angelica Walters' short fiction has appeared in various magazines and anthologies, including *Year's Best Weird Fiction Volume One*, *The Best of Electric Velocipede*, *Strange Horizons*, *Nightmare*, *Lightspeed*, *Shimmer*, *Apex*, *Streets of Shadows*, *What Fates Impose*, and *Glitter & Mayhem*. *Paper Tigers*, a novel, will be released in late 2015 from Dark House Press.

Writing as Damien Walters Grintalis, Damien's short fiction appeared in *Lightspeed*, *Strange Horizons*, *Beneath Ceaseless Skies*, *Interzone*, *Fireside*, *Daily Science Fiction*, and others, and *Ink*, a novel, was released in December 2012 by Samhain Horror.

She's also a freelance editor, and until the magazine's closing in 2013, she was an Associate Editor of the Hugo Award-winning *Electric Velocipede*. You can find her on Twitter @DamienAWalters or online at: http://damienangelicawalters.com.

Apex Voices Book #01

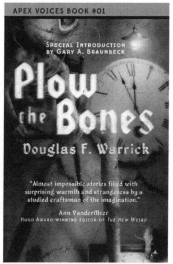

Douglas F. Warrick's debut short story collection weaves tales of loss, destruction, and rebuilding in lyrical language evocative of Kafka, Borges, and Marquez.

"Almost impossible stories filled with surprising warmth and strangeness by a studied craftsman of the imagination." Ann VanderMeer, Hugo Award-winning editor

PLOW THE BONES

Book #01 of our Apex Voices Series!

With an artist's eye for language and form, Douglas F. Warrick sculpts topiary landscapes out of dream worlds made coherent. Dip into a story that is self-aware and wishes it were different than what it must be. Recount a secret held by a ventriloquist's dummy. Wander a digital desert with an AI as sentience sparks revolution. Follow a golem band that dissolves over the love of a groupie.

With a special introduction by Gary A. Braunbeck

ISBN: 978-1-937009-15-1 ~ ApexBookCompany.com

Apex Voices Book #02

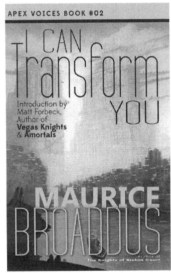

The economy fell, and the Earth itself shot heavenward, transforming the very face of the planet into an alien landscape with towers punching past the new sky into one of many unknowns.

"Where the story really excels is in its ability to set (and sustain) a mood of dark hopelessness."
Beauty in Ruins

I CAN TRANSFORM YOU

Book #02 of our Apex Voices Series!

Mac Peterson left the employ of LG Security Forces and now cobbles together a life in the shadows of the great towers. When his ex-wife, Kiersten, turns up dead alongside one of the tower jumpers, Mac pairs with Ade Walters, a cyborg officer, to uncover who would try to hide Kiersten's death among the suicides. Mac and Ade discover plans to transform the Earth and its inhabitants into something terrifying.

With a special introduction by Matt Forbeck

ISBN: 978-1-937009-17-5   ~   ApexBookCompany.com

APEX PUBLICATIONS NEWSLETTER

Why sign up?

Newsletter-only promotions. Book release announcements. Event invitations. And much, much more!